Love and Betrayal:
Part II
Loyalty Never Dies

A Novel By: R.J.G.

Reginald Gist

A T & P Publishing Book by arrangement with the author.

Printing History

First printing: October 2017

Copyright 2017 by Reginald Gist

Cover design and production by

ISBN: 978--0-9913581-3-7

Acknowledgements:

I would first like to acknowledge the all mighty God for giving me the talent and drive to pursue my dreams. I would also like to acknowledge my family who gave me the strength and motivation to complete this body of work. Last but not least, I would like to acknowledge all of those whom supported me throughout my struggles while building this brand....

R.J.G.

Dedications:

This novel is dedicated to all of those who have experienced true love in the most extreme ways. In life we're often faced with many options and sometimes we choose the wrong ones. We must remember that when we fail or fall to be sure that we land on our backs; therefore, it's easier for us to get back up. Stay true to yourself and value your relationships. If, relationships seem to scare you then always trust that an understanding is worth its weight in gold...

Chapter One

The weather is warm, the leaves are brown, and the sky is as clear as the tropical waters. Outside the huge backyard, Stacy plays catch with her two small children while Ms. Moore makes cold drinks. It has been three years since the death of her fiancé and best friend and her recovery is still a work in progress.

After several surgeries and therapy sessions, Stacy was released from the hospital while being four months pregnant. A lot weighed on her heart and mind during these days of her present goals. Shortly after giving birth to the twins, she was faced with yet another dilemma in her life. Trying to find out who the father of her twins was an emotional process.

Once the nurse at the clinic announced the results; Stacy's heart dropped four beats out of shock. The almost impossible had happened and these results would change Stacy's life forever. She was blessed with two healthy, loveable, children; one girl and one boy; but to her surprise, each child, although a miracle had a different father. Joetta was beautiful with eyes like her daddy Joey and Tyrik was very handsome with hair like his daddy Terrence.

The only obstacle she faced with the children was revealing these results to her family and friends. So, to keep tension down, she decided to keep it a secret and tell everyone that both babies were Joey's. After her recovery Stacy vowed to be a good mother and to never let her guard down again.

Out of fear and bad memories, Stacy relocated to a beautiful four-bedroom home in Canton, Michigan. Her business was still taking off financially and Joey's parents always demanded to play a major role. They would babysit and support along with Ms. Moore who enjoyed their company as well.

The thought of remaining in the same home that she and Joey once shared was not an option. Raising their children under the same roof that he was murdered in would be a lifetime curse. Instead, with the help of a family real estate agent, she found a home away from the past drama.

Things would be different now on all aspects. Living alone as a single parent would require a lot of time and countless energy. Thank God that Rondo had survived the shooting at the hospital and had vowed to be the Godparent to both children. While still in mourning along with Stacy, he would always stop by to make sure that they were okay. Rondo's recovery had been slow as he remained on crutches for several years.

Each night, Stacy would pray to give thanks to the Lord for allowing her to survive and learn from the choices that she had made. Over the last few years she had strived to re-strengthen her surroundings and health. By taking things day by day she would rebuild her brand while focusing on expanding her career. Her heart had still belonged to Joey and no man could ever compare to the love that she had for him. Losing him along with Kim who was viciously shot down at the hospital made it hard to welcome friends or associates.

While struggling to overcome the past events and health problems, Stacy vowed to stay under the radar to avoid all the local gossip. The entire family knew that she was the cause of all of the drama, but tried to let time pass to grow stronger.

Throughout the years life was hard and Stacy stayed strong to reassure her children a better future. Once a month and on special days they would all visit the grave of their loved ones along with her father. Strength is measured by faith and she knew that belief in the unseen is all that she had left.

One evening while playing with the kids she observed them gaining an identity when her phone rang with a call from Tee-Tee her new BFF. Stacy had heard the cell phone on the picnic table ringing as she ran to answer it.

"Hello?"

"Hey girl! What you doing?" Tee asked.

"Bout time you called girl. I'm at the house playing around with my babies. How was your trip?" she asked.

"It was nice honey, Rome really had shit laid out for me. We got back last night and I wanted to come and see my little ones," Tee-Tee stated.

"Of course. See you soon Sis," Stacy said while hanging up.

After continuing to entertain the kids for several hours, Tee-Tee pulled up in her new Porsche truck. They greeted each other with a quick hug then headed toward the backyard to see the children.

"Hey babies! Ya'll are so cute! Hello, Ms. Moore!" Tee-Tee spoke excitedly.

The children ran to meet her; Ms. Moore spoke back with a grin.

"Are you thirsty Tee? Ma made some daiquiris," Stacy asked politely.

"Sure, let's drink and catch up" she responded.

Shortly after grabbing the drinks they headed to the cool living room to talk for a few. "Hey what's on your mind, Tee?" Stacy joked.

"Well, when I came back from our trip; I was at the barbershop getting my nails done when I overheard some crazy news."

"Bout what?" Stacy asked.

"Tamika was telling Paris about Rondo setting off a beef against the entire eastside," Tee-Tee said worried.

"Why would he do some stupid shit like that?" Stacy responded.

"I guess since he's better, he wants revenge for Joey, Kim, and himself."

"Shit, the streets about to be on fire, Tee. I can't support any shit like that, especially having my babies and business in the hood," Stacy stated angrily.

"You need to lay low until we get the real scoop. Don't tell Rondo that I said anything because then Rome will be all on my back for talking too much," Tee-Tee pleaded.

"You straight girl, but I'm going to call his crazy ass to talk to him later," Stacy said rolling her eyes.

After talking for half an hour they decided to go back outside to enjoy the weather and the children. Tee-Tee loved being a friend; and true supporter of the family. Telling Stacy the gossip was only to help keep her alert of the dangers that could lie ahead. Since Stacy wasn't in tune with the streets anymore, Tee-Tee made sure that she was always up to date.

As they entered the yard, both children rushed Tee-Tee and requested that she get a little dirty by playing in the sandbox. While she did what they requested, Stacy stepped over to the picnic table to call Rondo.

"What it do?" Rondo said as he picked up the phone.

"Hey boy, what's the deal with you?" She jugged at him.

"Shit, just about to head over to pick up Doc to hit up Hard Body's for a quick drink," he responded calmly.

"The kids asked about you and are you still going to help me with their party planning?" she questioned.

"Yeah, girl you straight," Rondo replied. "Tell them I said I love them and I'll fall through Saturday to see them."

"Cool and I also heard about you wanting to holler at them other dudes too, Rondo," she pushed.

"Dig Shorty, only thing you gotta know is don't talk over the phone and don't panic. I'm out here in these fucking streets 24/7 and if I don't send a message then that means I accept my position as prey. Never forget that my best friend and yours are gone over a simple misjudgment call," He stated aggressively.

"See, now you blaming me again Rondo. It's always put the drama on Stacy. We don't need a war; we need a solution crazy ass!"

"I feel ya and I got it. Relax and let me do the thinking okay. I gotta go, but we'll catch up Saturday, cool?" he asked.

"Yeah, alright, be careful stupid ass," she joked as they both hung up.

Back outside Tee-Tee played with the kids as Ms. Moore shouted out "lunch time!" They all ran to greet her at the table, but not before she demanded that they wash their hands.

In the corner chair Stacy sat daydreaming about her past. This is something that she always did growing up.

"Hey, are you okay?" Tee-Tee asked catching her off guard.

"Oh, Oh yeah, I'm okay, girl. Just thinking about some old shit."

"Do we need to talk?" Tee asked.

"Nah, I'm cool, just thinking about Rondo crazy ass and missing Joey and Kim," Stacy stated.

"Yeah, I know missy. Well I gotta get home to catch Rome before he leaves to go to Vegas."

"Alright be sure to call me when you get home and don't forget about the kid's party Saturday."

"I won't. See you later and you'll be okay girl."

"Thanks Tee. Call me," Stacy said while hugging her goodbye.

Once she left the house Stacy relaxed in the soft wicker lounge chair to enjoy a little bit of the sun. Being on edge was never a feeling she liked, so instead she allowed her thoughts to drift off into a place of comfort. Reminiscing about Joey and the times they shared always brought her to tears of joy. No man could ever love her the way he had and all she had to show for it was their daughter...

Chapter Two

After several days of hustling non-stop, Rondo had set up a meeting with his crew to discuss their next move. Over the last few years he had become a powerful member of the Fenkell Boyz Crew. Immediately, after Joey's death, his dad, Mr. A, had placed him amongst the ranked members so Rondo then reached out to his partner in crime Doc. Even though Doc was from a different hood, his loyalty lied with the person who had his best interest at heart. The two did everything together as a team and when Joey was alive he loved his company as well.

Doc wore medium-length dreads in his hair and was 6 feet even and 175 pounds. When Rondo was shot five times Doc stayed by his side the entire time at the hospital. During the rehabilitation sessions; he also played a major role and this brought their bond to a new level. Rondo loved him like a brother and trusted him with his life.

As they all sat down at the round table, Rondo began giving his orders. "Listen, those motherfuckers killed our family! Then shot me five times along with Kim!" he shouted banging on the large table. "I had to walk around with a shit bag and crutches all over some bullshit," he added angry.

"So, what we gone do family?" Doc asked seriously.

"We gone wage a war against every motherfucker east of Woodward. They can't eat, sleep, or hustle without paying the price. We gotta send a message that we're serious about the loss of our homeboy!" he stated hyper.

A few of the guys in the room were all for the idea while others were not. However, no one voiced their opinion because no one wanted to look weak or disloyal. Instead they nodded their heads in approval and awaited the last commands.

"So fam, you want us to shoot on sight?" Doc asked.

"No, not yet. I need all y'all to search for a black S.U.V. with tinted windows and paper tags in the rear window. Then bring me the information or the driver alive," he demanded.

"Alright everybody hit the streets because project flush a nigga out is in full affect," Doc spoke with a light grin.

All the soldiers headed out to fulfill their duties as Rondo sat back and phoned Stacy.

"What's up Rondo?" she answered out of breath.

"Shit, how the kids?" he asked.

"They out back enjoying the party."

"I'll be out there to drop their gifts off shortly, you need anything?" he politely asked.

"Nah, I'm cool," she replied.

"Alright catch ya in a few," he said before hanging up.

Today was the twin's birthday and as their God dad he wanted to surprise them. Days prior he had arranged to have two puppies dropped off along with two twin electric Mobile cars. As a bonus gift, he would bring sponge bob and friends with him to have a sing along.

When he pulled up to the house everyone greeted him as if he was family. The children loved to play with Rondo and he could always see J-rock in their eyes and personalities. After a few hours of eating cake and playing games, the day was coming to a slow end.

Stacy had asked him to follow her into the den to talk for a second, "Listen, I'm not trying to be all in your business, but this war you started can mean major trouble."

"And?" he spoke.

"We don't need this, me and the kids don't want to lose you. You're our family," Stacy cried.

Rondo listened to every word, but felt no change of heart toward the war. Deep down inside he was still bitter about her actions that led to all of the drama. Forgiving her was something that he could do, but forgetting was something he didn't do. "Let me handle the streets, my loyalty is with my homie who lays 6-feet under outta jealousy. His death and Kim's must be revenged Stacy. They tried to kill you also, are you forgetting?" he asked with raised eyebrows.

"I know but…"

He cut her off quickly. "But nothing, they played for keeps so must we. You'll be ok trust me. Just let me be me," he demanded.

"Okay. I'm through" she said to avoid any further arguing. His mind was made up and his orders were etched in stone.

Shortly after the party he said his good-byes as Stacy prepared the children for bed. While driving away into the sunset he thought about the road that lied ahead.

The next day at the office, Rondo got a call from his wing man Doc. "What up fam?" Rondo answered.

"Dig, got a little info from my eastside bitch," Doc stated.

"Cool, meet you at the spot in 20 minutes," he replied and hung up. Twenty minutes later they sat at the small table drinking a bottle of Piper's. This table at the back of Starter's Bar & Grill was their favorite hangout.

"Alright, talk to me," Rondo demanded.

"Dig, my little chic Terry hit me and told me about the dude in the black truck. She said that he's been trying to get at her for the longest. His name is Tone and he used to work for Big-T as a hit man. He got a spot pumping blow over on Brentwood!" Doc spoke excitedly.

"Yeah, that's good fam. Put together a team and y'all hit that spot and find this nigga," Rondo responded smiling.

They then relaxed enjoyed a quick meal before exiting the crowded bar. Outside they shook hands and parted ways until after the mission was done.

Back in the hood, Doc assembled three dudes from the crew to make the hit on Tone's spot. Dressed in tore up clothing and driving a stolen Chevy, they headed to the eastside of Detroit. Each member had specific instructions once they arrived; each member also had new throw away pistols.

Moments later they pulled up to the solid brick house dressed like dope fiends. One of the dudes knocked at the door to be let in to purchase drugs.

"What you need nigga?" the young cocky dude spoke.

"Ahhh, can I get a 50 playa?" Doc asked.

The young dude turned to tell another worker to fetch a $50 pack off the fireplace. Seconds later Doc pulled out his 357 revolver and pointed it at both workers before they could reach for their weapons.

"STOP NIGGAS! DON'T FUCKING MOVE OR YA DEAD!!!!" He demanded loudly.

They both stood shaking in their spots as Doc chirped his device to the others waiting in the car, "Let's get it we're clear," he shouted. Then he opened the door to let them in while the other crew members kept the car running.

"Both of y'all get the fuck on the floor!" they demanded.

"Now, we got two options here! Y'all can tell me where Tone is or die trying to be loyal!" Doc said.

Immediately they sang like church girls on Sunday mornings, while the two crew members searched the entire house. Once the workers gave up Tone's stash house and all the dope and money was seized, Doc gave the signal to end their lives instantly. Just like that, both boys were shot in the back of the head, and left to die in a puddle of their own blood.

As time stood still the Fenkell Boyz had all they needed as they headed back West to talk to Rondo. On the way to the hood Doc called to give him the news.

"Good looking fam" Rondo said.

"It ain't shit my dude, what's next?" Doc asked wondering.

"Drop the car and yo niggas off. Let them keep the money and drugs then meet me at spot B," he instructed.

"Gotcha fam, see ya in 30 minutes," Doc chuckled then hung up.

An hour after the hit on the blow house, they met up at Doll House Bar to talk. They discussed the new information they received and made plans to catch up with Tone this weekend.

With the info Rondo and Doc received they used it to set up surveillance on Tone's house. For several days, they watched him come and leave unnoticed. He was a heavy-set dude with brush waves and huge muscles. This would pose as a challenge to both men who were much smaller than the attended victim.

After observing his place in Downtown Detroit they noticed that this wasn't just a stash house. The location that they visited was actually his home front. On Saturday morning before the planned hit, Doc realized that inside the house was a child and older female. As a family, they all headed out together to barbecue at Belle Isle Park.

He watched and followed their every move then reported it back to Rondo via cell phone. "Dog check, I was doing my thing on ole boy and seen that this his main crib," Doc explained.

"So?" Rondo replied.

"Man we can't fuck with the family fam," Doc said discouraged.

"So?" Rondo stated.

"Man we can't fuck with the family fam," Doc spoke looking lost.

"Understand this, that nigga killed Kim and tried to kill me. In war, there are no guidelines or morals. So, if we must do his family then it's just another causality of war," Rondo spoke calmly sitting in his chair.

"I gottcha, you my man and I'm wit ya 100 percent," Doc reassured him.

"Good, get the car ready because I'm going on this mission by myself, "Rondo ordered.

"Oh no nigga! We'll go together."

"Yeah ok."

"Meet you at the club house at 10 pm sharp," Doc suggested.

Several hours later at 10:30pm, the two set in the stolen Mustang parked across from Tone's home downtown. Smoking on a blunt and black and mild they waited to build up the nerves to kick in the door. Neither one wanted to harm the woman and child, but life wasn't promised to anyone.

As they prepared to exit the vehicle, Tone opened up the front door getting ready to leave the house. Seconds later, he turned to say goodbye to his family and grabbed several small bags. This gave Doc enough time to jump out the Mustang and rush to the parked SUV parked on the street. Instantly, he stopped, dropped, and rolled under the large truck to wait for his victim.

Moments afterwards, Tone closed the door to the house and headed towards the truck. In full stride he deactivated the alarm with intentions on entering quickly. Suddenly, as Tone reached for the truck door handle, Doc rolled from up under the truck with the pistol aimed. Quickly Rondo came across the street and placed his gun to the back of Tone's head.

"Don't move motherfucker," Rondo whispered.

Tone was caught off guard and froze in his tracks. "W-W what's this shit?" Tone asked nervously.

"SHUT THE FUCK UP AND OPEN THE DAMN DOOR!!!" Doc yelled while jumping up from the ground.

Rondo pushed him into the truck as Tone complied with the orders.

"What's this about nigga?" Tone asked again.

"Listen nigga, you know the deal. You know why I'm here," Rondo reassured.

"Who are you? I can't see your face," Tone cried.

At this point Rondo took off of his mask to reveal his face. "Ohhh shit!" Tone yelled.

"Now, tell me why you tried to kill me and you only got 5 seconds!" Rondo demanded.

"5-4-3.." Doc started counting while holding his pistol to Tone's head.

"I-I-I can explain please wait!"

"Go on," Rondo ordered.

"Uh-uh the hit was a contract," Tone stated.

"Go on," Rondo ordered.

"It came from Rickey as a message to Kim. It wasn't attended for you at all," Tone spoke out of fear.

"Yeah, but it involved me and SHE WAS MY FRIEND!!!" Rondo yelled while smacking him with the barrel of the gun.

"Oh shit, I'm bleeding nigga! Chill out!" Tone yelled as blood dripped down his cheek unto the leather truck seats.

"Where the fuck is this nigga Ricky at??" Doc shouted.

"He-He-He lives in Miami, but he'll be here in a few months to celebrate Big-T's death date," Tone replied.

"Oh yeah," Doc spoke.

"Come on man this beef isn't about me, dog. I told y'all everything. I got a wife and kid," Tone pleaded.

While Rondo asked questions, Doc scanned the street to see if any traffic or neighbors were around.

"Why was Kim a target?" Rondo asked angrily.

"Man, Rick wanted payback since she hooked Stacy up with Big-T. We didn't know anyone else close to Stacy, but her. We never knew that you were there or if Stacy survived," Tone said.

While Rondo continued to question Tone for information. Doc reached over Rondo's shoulder and fired 3 shots into Tone's head; killing him instantly.

"WHAT THE FUCK!!!!" Rondo screamed.

"Let's go nigga, we out!" Doc demanded.

Once in the car, they sped towards the Westside quickly.

"Dog, why you shoot the nigga?" Rondo asked.

"He was talking too much, plus it would only be a matter of time before his girl noticed that the truck hadn't left," Doc explained.

"How the hell is we gone find Ricky ass now?" Rondo asked.

"Easily, we'll just keep our eyes open for the party for Big-T. We already know the day he died," Doc responded.

"You a crazy nigga, fam," Rondo joked.

"I know, let's ditch this shit and lay low," Doc said.

On the way to ditch the ride they made plans to hit the bar to celebrate. Then it would be operation 'Kill Ricky' A.S.A.P...

Chapter Three

In Miami, Ricky laid in his bed at the condo he owned, overlooking the port of Miami. It's 8:30 a.m. and his cell phone rings with a call from Jeff. Jeff is a captain of his crew who lives in Detroit, but originated from Miami.

"Speak," Ricky answers.

"Hey, Fammo is the line secure?" Jeff asked.

"Yeah, we good, what's the problem?" Ricky asked back.

"Man shit crazy down here and a lot of stupid shit is affecting the business," Jeff said.

"Like what?"

"I got a call from Keisha this morning crying about Tone getting killed in front of her house," says Jeff.

"WHAT!!!" Ricky shouted.

"Yeah it's all over the news and everything," Jeff stated.

"What happened?" Ricky asked.

"They say he was shot several times inside the truck, that's it," Jeff said.

"Damn, that's my dude fam. Dig, send money for the funeral from me then check out that Rondo guy information," Ricky demanded.

"I already got it Cuz. He's been out of recovery for about six months and he's running ole boy's business and crew," said Jeff.

"Yeah," Ricky said. "I betcha he playing on get back terms too," said Ricky.

"Probably so."

"Don't worry I'm sending a team to the "D" in the morning. Call ya later," Ricky said as he hung up.

Immediately he woke up to prepare for a long day of assembling a hit squad to seek retaliation. The hit he had placed on Kim had come back to haunt him and in due time things would reveal. Gathering several members of the "Zone Pound Crew" and sending them to Detroit wouldn't be easy.

After calling multiple associates and planning a full fledge attack, it was finally time to call Jeff back.

"What it do my guy?" Jeff answered.

"Four to come, meet at the warehouse and supply all that they need" Ricky spoke then hung up, while Jeff calmly arranged for the transportation and firearms to help aid in the attack on the Fenkell Boys. Ricky had felt confident that Rondo was out for revenge and that his team would deliver.

Over the next few days he would sit and await the results so that business could get back to normal. The next morning Jeff had got a call from Tik and Vaughn alerting him of their arrival. They met up and discussed the plans to take out Rondo.

"Give me what you got on the guy," Tik demanded.

Jeff had been studying Rondo over the past few years along with Tone. They watched him recover from the shooting along with Stacy who slipped off the radar somehow. Jeff knew everything about him, his work and his hangouts. The only thing he couldn't figure out was his place of residence.

"Here you go fam and this is a picture of him and his wingman," Jeff noted.

"Cool, let's go to work. We'll need you to drive us around the city," Vaughn said.

"Anything you need, I gotcha," Jeff responded.

Along with several other crew members, Jeff, Tik and Vaughn headed out to search for the intended target. They wanted to waste no time so that the out of town hit men could get away without being noticed.

Prior to waiting for the hit squad to make it to Detroit, Jeff had set up a tail on Rondo the night before to aid in the search. Grabbing his mobile he contacted his captain who was hot on the tail of Rondo.

"Talk to me" the large built captain spoke through the cell. "What's the 411 on my dude?" Jeff asked.

"Shit, J-Rizzle we got him up here at Chili's with some dread head dude in Dearborn," the captain said.

"Dig stay there, we are on our way to relieve you," Jeff said anxiously.

Exactly 30 minutes later they pulled up as Rondo was inside ordering his dessert.

"Imma go in to check shit out. When they exit to head to their car, that's when we'll take them out," Tik ordered.

As Rondo and Doc sat inside the restaurant talking they realized that it was time to leave. They talked and joked while walking to the car not knowing that they were being followed. Outside, the hit squad waited patiently for the right time to pounce on the two.

Fortunately, Rondo always walked with his gun in hand when approaching his car. It was a lesson well learned along with the demo that led to Tone's death.

Deactivating the alarm to the car and initiating the automatic start was routine. Suddenly, out of the corner of his eye Doc noticed a slim light skinned dude creeping fast.

"Watch this nigga, Ron," Doc said.

As soon as the words left his mouth, they saw a gun appear in one of his hands. The stranger released several shots from his weapon as Doc and Rondo ran for cover. Doc pulled out his hand gun while diving next to the car. Him and Rondo exchanged shots with the men as they noticed several dudes jumping out of a blue Charger. The men opened fire on them in broad daylight.

"Doc, get in the car!" Rondo yelled.

At this point Doc climbed into the car while Rondo fired his last few rounds from behind the small van. The hit squad tried to close them in with rapid fire and by blocking off their car. Instead Doc put the car in drive as Rondo jumped in quickly. Doc pushed the pedal to the floor and rear ended the Charger spinning it into circles.

The hit squad continued to fire upon the moving car tearing chunks of metal and fiber glass away.

"Get out of here! It's a hit!" Rondo yelled over the gun fire.

"You straight nigga?" Doc yelled back.

"Yeah, what the fuck is going on?" Rondo questioned.

As they pulled away escaping the ambush, the hit squad gave chase briefly. Once they saw the Dearborn Police speeding toward the scene; they respectfully aborted the mission.

"Damn man!" Tik yelled.

"We fucking missed!" Vaughn shouted.

The men in the Charger were irritated from the lack of success on the hit. Jeff decided to take them to the hide out until orders came from Ricky on the next move. He knew that Ricky would be in town in a few weeks and wanted things to be settled before his arrival. Picking up the cell he then phoned him from the car.

"Talk," Ricky answered.

"We missed fam," Jeff whispered.

"Stupid Motherfuckers!" Ricky yelled angrily.

"Don't worry we'll get him!" Vaughn shouted in the background.

"Shut the fuck up! Now he knows we're on to him, the element of surprise is gone!" Ricky stated. "Everyone lay low until after the party. Bye," again he spoke before hanging up.

Meanwhile, Doc and Rondo had found refuge at a nearby friend's house in Dearborn. Doc had a few women located throughout the city, as did Rondo. While shaking off the jitters and refocusing on the problem; Kyra fixed them a drink and blunt to calm them down.

"Man, this shit crazy! We can't get caught slipping Ron!" Doc said.

"This nigga Ricky getting on my fucking nerves, we got to off this dude!" Rondo stated.

While sitting in the living room; Kyra overheard their conversation. "Y'all already know I'm nosy as hell.

Are y'all talking about short cocky Ricky from Miami?"
Kyra asked cautiously.

"Damn, Bitch! You all in a nigga mouth!" Doc stated.

Kyra was not upset by his actions at all. She had been on his team for years and was as ruthless and coldhearted as any man. "Don't forget this is my house stupid ass!" she responded smiling.

"Y'all crazy as hell!" Rondo joked.

"Anyway, I know that nigga real good and he invited me and a few girls to the after party next Saturday," she spoke.

"What after party?" Doc asked.

"You know his boy killed himself over some broad a few years ago. So, every year he throws a gone away party for his friends and family. They got a secret spot where the after party is at and need us to dance for them," she explained.

"Real talk?" Rondo responded.

"Yeah nigga, I got to get my cash on! Dude pay two grand a night and five grand if you fucking," she said.

"How about I give you 10-grand to tell me where the after party is at?" Rondo asked.

"It sounds good Rondo, but he only tells us where it's at an hour prior. Plus, there are no cell phones allowed and we're searched before we enter," Kyra spoke.

"Damn, he on his shit, man" Doc said out loud.

For a few minutes they sat around and smoked until the marijuana gave them several ideas.

"Tell ya what, since the location is a secret how about I do the hit for y'all?" Kyra suggested.

"Can you handle that, girl?" Doc asked. "Boy how many plays have we put down on nigga's? You doubting me?" she joked.

After several hours of thinking, the plan was set in motion. Next, Rondo and Doc cleaned themselves up while the car was towed to the local shop. Afterwards, they got a few rental cars to stay under the radar in the hood and they continued to hustle until the party.

Back on the eastside Jeff waited for more orders from Ricky as he planned for the party next weekend. The entire city was at war, while many others prepared to mourn the death of a fallen soldier.

Throughout the city, flyers floated around inviting everyone to attend the big bash. Tee-Tee had grabbed a few from the barbershop and showed them to Stacy over lunch. "Girl, this party is about to be crazy as hell!" Tee-Tee stated.

"I know, it's crazy. The entire city blame me for this shit," Stacy said shaking her head slow.

"Don't let this get you down girl. We all make mistakes in life, we just gotta learn from them. We know you loved Joey and Terrance was just a fling. Shit you did tell him in the long-run, he just couldn't accept it. Stacy you might have some killa pussy, but you didn't pull no trigga" Tee-Tee spoke.

"I know it's just sad to be in this place in my life. I miss Joey soooo much," Stacy said while tears flowed down her face.

Tee-Tee stood up to hug her in comfort and to show support. After their lunch, the both of them separated ways to continue with their day. Tee-Tee hated to see her best-friend in the state that she was in and vowed to pay close attention to her.

Meanwhile, several days had flown past and it was time for a big celebration. Ricky was in town as the host of the bash, while Jeff and the hit squad played security.

On the other side of town Rondo and Doc relaxed and waited for the phone call from Kyra. They had the location to the party, but decided not to crash it due to tight security. The event was a full-blown celebration. They had huge portraits of Big-T throughout the club with a high-profile guest list. Celebrities from all over came to support; including Cash Money Records.

Even though this was the second party, the crowd was still filled with A-listers and close associates. Steve's Soul Food Restaurant supplied the food while D.J. Funk master Flex entertained the crowded club. Champagne and exotic marijuana smoke filled the jam-packed event, as everyone celebrated the lost life of Terrance.

After several hours of partying, it was getting close to the club's closing time. Ricky and Jeff and the crew gathered up selected females who fitted the criteria of money getters. By Kyra being the ring leader of majority of the girls, Jeff approached her to bring in a few to the after spot. The location was unknown and each female would be searched and placed on a party bus for travel.

Kyra was 5ft 7inches, 165lbs, with a body like "Buffy the Body." Ricky had tried several times before to get her to trick with him, but since she was cool with Kim she declined. Excepting the offer this time had Ricky a little alert, but he still allowed her to participate. Kyra was sexy and sneaky which made her a little bit dangerous.

Days before the party she had purchased a stolen 45. Lima the size of a pants pocket. Then she had a pair of her favorite Chanel boots cut on the inside and re-stuffed with extra padding. This would allow her to slip the small gun holding 13 shots into a secret side pocket. Coming prepared was something she took for granted while very few didn't. With the boots ready to pass a major pat down the mission would be a success.

Later that night Jeff rounded up all the females that were available for the night. Once he contacted Ricky, he gave them directions to the loft in Southfield. The loft was a beautiful brick building equipped with a bar and two stripper poles. There were large couches, pool tables, a pool, and several rooms to separate from the action.

The bus arrived at 2:30am as the 12 females entered the loft ready to party and hustle. Ricky sat on the couch in the center of the room drinking a bottle of Remy XO.

"Welcome to one of my humble abodes," he joked.

Jeff, Tik, and Vaughn all gave him high fives as they scanned the room.

"This shit nice dog. I like this set up," Jeff said.

"Yeah, I had this for a while and it has a secret getaway tunnel," Ricky said drunkenly.

"Well we got 3 dudes on the ground and everyone was searched before we left the club," Jeff said.

"O.K. let the hoes in and let's do this for my nigga Big-T!!!!" Ricky yelled.

Jeff opened the door to invite all 12 women in to earn all the money they needed. While Ricky oversaw each female's exotic entrance, he noticed Kyra looking very seductive. "Oh, you made it huh?" he asked jokingly.

"Of course, honey, why wouldn't I? She responded.

"You've been avoiding a nigga for years 'K'. No more Kim now you game for a change," he slurred.

"Respect to my friends is a must, plus a bitch gotta eat ya know," she said smiling.

Tik took it upon himself to plug his IPad up to the huge system operated by Bose Surround Sounds. Putting the IPad on random selected songs, the girls began to dance for the 30 plus members at the VIP gathering.

"Damn, can I dance for you?" Kyra asked.

Ricky looked amazed as she peeled out of her body suit into a thong and no bra. Kyra knew that in order to complete the mission that she had to stay close to Ricky and observe the surroundings.

"Dig, Vaughn, grab that suitcase out the back and let's show these hoes how we do it in Miami," Ricky spoke loudly.

Vaughn left to return seconds later with a suitcase holding $150,000 cash inside. The women all noticed as Ricky pulled out stacks and peeled off $50 and $100 bills to stuff into Kyra thongs. A crowd of women all rushed to aid in the private dance, only to be eye balled by away.

To lighten up the tension, Ricky passed out stacks to the crew with orders to tip and fuck every one of the groupies.

As Kyra danced she quickly viewed all the men being tended to and counted all the bodies. On the way into the loft she also noticed a bathroom with a pull up window on the first floor. She also noticed 3 armed men posted at the front and side doors. Once the hit was done her getaway would be harder than she thought.

"Damn, you gotta fat ass and pussy, K," Ricky stated.

The comments he made over the loud music snapped Kyra out of her mental planning. "Yeah nigga, you better believe it," she smirked.

After several dances and an hour later, she asked to be excused to scan the room. "I'll be back, Ricky let some of these other hoes dance for you baby," she stated.

Ricky smiled as he inhaled the weed and scanned the room for something nice. While many of the crew members were busy fucking and enjoying the view of the many rooms. Kyra strolled through the loft doing a final check through before the big moment. Once everything was mapped out and everyone was busy, she made her move.

"O.K. baby I'm back," she said.

"Bout time, girl," Ricky said.

"You look kinda high Ricky," Kyra whispered in his ear.

"Naww just ready to fuck, ya dig" he responded calmly.

"Let's get it. I'll follow you boo," she said sexily.

Ricky stood up and ordered several guys to stay alert as he left the room. He had a special spot in the house where he would take females. This room had the secret crawl space that led to a tunnel which exited into the small garage.

Once they entered the room Kyra made Ricky lay on the bed after he undressed. Slowly she started to dance exotic as he watched and waited for her to slip out of her thong. Ricky was drunk and barely aware of his surroundings due to sex on the brain. As soon as she bent over to let him see her from behind; she reached for the boot that obtained the hidden weapon. Retrieving the gun unnoticed, she then aimed it at Ricky who lay watching her every move.

Kyra let off several shots at him hitting him in the arm and shoulder as he rolled off the bed. With the lights off, she gave chase firing shots all around the bed. Too late, to her surprise Ricky had slid under the bed to the crawl space to get away.

"Shit!" Kyra yelled. Seconds later she knew that she had to make an immediate exit.

Outside the room Tik had walked past to head into the lavish den. Upon arriving the sounds of gun shots muffled the area. Quickly he became alert as he rushed to check on Ricky. With gun in hand he prepared to enter the secret room for observation.

Kyra timed the entrance exactly, as she kicked the door knocking Tik off balance while still firing her gun.

"Shit Bitch!!! Tik shouted as he was hit in the leg and lower stomach. Falling to the ground, he returned shots that he thought had to hit her somewhere. Drifting out of conscience he passed out from the pain and wounds.

Kyra ran through the house shooting at everyone to cause a major commotion. The distraction allowed her time to locate the bathroom downstairs and jump through the window. While she attempted her leap of faith, several guys outside rushed inside to secure Ricky. This was the perfect time to jump and head for the car she had trail her to the party. Seconds later as she reached the parked car, gunshots rang throughout the secluded area. Multiple bullets hit the vehicle shattering the fiber optic frame of the small Malibu.

Inside the car sat Akia, a close friend of hers and Doc. Thank God, he had her to trail the bus just in case things got crazy. Immediately they took off heading for Dearborn as the gunshots faded into the thin air of the early morning...

Chapter Four

Back in Canton, Stacy had been trying her best to avoid any drama by staying busy. Several days before the party of Terrance, she lay on her bed looking at the flyer reminiscing about her past. Day dreaming was the only way that she found peace in her heart and mind.

Sometimes thinking about Joey and Terrance was hard and painful. Deep down she knew that no one could ever have her heart 100 percent. Over the past few years she had struggled with dating because everyone had to be compared to Joey. Changing this habit would take a long time and patience. 'Could she ever get through life?' she would lay and think until the sounds of children running woke her up.

"Mommy, Mommy!" they yelled.

"What's the matter? Calm down, dang!" she responded.

"Grandma said-said ahhh-ahhh Ms. Tee-Tee coming over," they spoke excitedly.

"O.K. baby, thank you," she said.

"You wwwel-come" Tyrik said smiling.

A few minutes later Tee-Tee pulled up to the house to visit. Walking into the living room the kids rushed as usual to greet her with hugs and kisses.

"Where ya mama at?" she asked.

Ms. Moore came out the kitchen to answer her and to say hello. "Hey Tee, she in the den laying down, gone back, you're alright" she said.

"Thank you, Ms. Moore. See y'all in a few o.k.?" Tee-Tee stated.

The kids went back to playing on the V-Tech computer that Rondo had brought months prior.

"Hey, sis?" Tee-Tee joked.

"See you finally made it," Stacy smiled.

Once they greeted with a hug, Tee-Tee could tell that Stacy had something on her mind.

"What's the matter lady?" Tee-Tee questioned.

"I'm cool, just been doing a lot of thinking about my life," Stacy replied.

"It's ok to think about the past. You've been through a lot over the last few years and you got the scars to prove it," Tee said.

"I know but it's hard raising two children alone," Stacy said.

"Of course it is girl, and in time your benefits will come," Tee said.

"My kids are 5years old now and they're starting to ask a lot of questions," Stacy said.

"About what? They're kids, girl," Tee-Tee asked strangely.

"Who is their daddy and talk like that hurts me," Stacy said.

"They had a wonderful daddy, so be proud of who he was," Tee-Tee stated.

At this point Stacy wanted to confess to her new BFF, that the twins had different fathers, but instead chose not to do so. This secret could change a lot of things for the better or worse if leaked into the wrong ears.

"You are right, but how do you think they would feel about me dating?" Stacy asked.

"They're kids; all they know is what you tell them. You'll have a harder time trying to convince the nigga that you're dating that it's cool. A lot of guys fear fucking with you cause of Joey. Then again true love will enter your life again, you'll see, you just gotta be ready," Tee-Tee smiled and said.

"I love you girl, you sure know how to make a bitch feel better!" Stacy joked back.

After talking about so much they prepared to do what Tee-Tee came over for anyhow. Rounding up the kids they began to focus on the 30-minute trip to view the grave sites of Joey and Kim. This routine was done regularly and Tee-Tee always came along to show support. By both of them being buried in Redford this process was always emotional and comforting.

Arriving at the cemetery everyone got set to check in while Stacy brought a few dozen flowers. The kids were familiar with this location, but as they got older the more they questioned things.

As Stacy prayed over the large headstone of Joey's she rearranged the flowers from oldest to newest. Tee-Tee entertained the kids by teaching them about life and death while allowing Stacy time to heal alone.

"Damn baby, I miss you sooo much. I'm so sorry that your life had to end due to me. I need you so bad and your daughter does too. I hope that she doesn't grow up to hate me Joey. She looks and acts just like your bossy ass. Huh, only if you were here baby, I love you," she said in a soft voice from crying; seconds later the children ran up to her to give hugs and kisses.

"Mommy, why you cry?" Tyrik asked worried.

"It's okay sweetie, mommy was just talking to daddy," Stacy stated.

"Okay, let's say goodbye to Daddy and go say bye-bye to Kim too," Tee-Tee suggested.

As the children rubbed the headstones and laid their flowers over it, Stacy looked on still crying. This was difficult to watch especially knowing that Tyrik wasn't Joey's son. At some point it would only be right to allow Terrance to meet his son along with his family. Time would only dictate these measures of maturity. There was still a lot that had to be revealed and explained and Stacy just wasn't ready to confess yet. Until then life would have to go on as planned with her keeping a vital secret close to her heart.

Since it was getting late Tee-Tee had to convince everyone that it was time to head home. So slowly they parted from the cemetery with promises to return again soon...

Chapter Five

In the car Kyra rested in the back seat as she noticed two gunshot wounds. "Ahhhh shit! Akia, I'm hit!" Kyra shouted.

"I'll jump on the freeway to the hospital, don't panic!" Akia spoke.

"Ahhh this shit hurt! That nigga shot me in my back and fucking leg," Kyra stated.

"Are you going to be alright?" Akia questioned.

"Yeah, but damn I missed that nigga Ricky! Shit call Doc for me," she demanded.

While driving down the freeway Akia dialed Doc number to confirm the latest news.

"Hello, what's up?" Doc answered as him and Rondo watch the Channel 4 news.

"I'm in the car with Kay-Kay and she got shot a few times!" Akia said.

"Is she alright?" he asked.

"I don't know she's in a lot of pain," Akia said.

"Did she complete the job?" he asked.

"No, he got away through some trap door or something like that," Akia explained.

"SHIT, SHIT, SHIT," Doc shouted.

"What up?" Rondo asked sitting across from Doc in the stash house.

"She's shot and the nigga got away," Doc explained to Rondo.

"Man, I knew we shouldn't send that hoe to do a man's job!" Rondo stated.

"Take her to Dr. Pickens on Davidson; he'll fix her up. I'll call to let him know the deal," Doc confirmed then hung up.

Once the call was finished Akia did as directed while the boys conversed.

"Dog, she needs to lay low for a while and watch her ass closely you hear me?" Rondo demanded.

"Yeah fam, my bad on the foul play," Doc responded.

"Next time it's on you for all mistakes; this is real life lil bro and mistakes will get us killed. Only because she's your girl will she be allowed to stay alive," Rondo spoke seriously.

"I know Ron, I gottcha fam," Doc reminded.

Meanwhile, several days later in Miami, Ricky lied in the bed recovering from a shot to the shoulder. On the couch in the living room Tik suffers from two shots to the thigh and left rib area.

"Fuck! I can't believe that bitch shot me! I know I popped her ass Ricky," Tik spoke.

"Yeah, hopefully ya did. I gotta admit, I never saw that coming," Ricky laughed in pain.

"We had the security search them and everything," Tik stated confused. "Somehow shit went wrong. How did you manage the getaway my people?" Tik asked, anxious to know.

"Thank God I saw her from behind messing with her big ass boots. I thought she wanted to take them off for me, and then I thought why, she's in a thong only. Once she danced her way to her boots again, I could see the chrome of the pistol. So, I tried to roll to the floor. Before you know it, she started shooting wildly. As I fell to the floor, I rolled under the bed to the open crawl space that led to the back wall and down to the garage," Ricky explained.

"Damn fam, you were on some James Bond type shit, huh?" Tik joked.

"Hell yeah, payback a motherfucker ya hear me?" Ricky said nodding.

Moments later the doorbell to the condo rang several times alerting everyone in the home. "Yo Ricky the fam here!!!" the huge guy on security yelled.

Before he agreed to let anyone in, Ricky yelled to his baby moms, brother, and son. Once they came from the back patio he told them to leave due to the squad meeting he scheduled. With promises to catch them later at the house, they all exited through the back elevator until later. Ricky's son, who was 6-years old, waved bye as the security guard waited for his next orders.

"Let them in," Ricky demanded. The six men entered the room all bearing some sort of get well soon gift. As they greeted each other with their special handshake, they all sat down to discuss business.

"Well, as you all know, there was a hit put on me in Detroit last week," Ricky stated.

Everyone looked surprised as the room got silent from grief.

"Do we know who did it?" one of the dudes asked.

"Of course, here is a picture of the dude name Rondo. He is an affiliate of a local crew called the Fenkell Boyz and is also the best friend of the dude Big-T killed. Out of revenge for the hit I put on Kim; he's been actively trying to kill me. The hit was never intended for him at all, but it is costing us a lot. Now the next order is to flush him out to end this shit. We have a profitable business in Detroit and need to stay focused," Ricky said seriously.

"What's the plan fam?" Tik asked anxiously.

"Since Jeff and Vaughn are still running the eastside crews, we'll start a killing spree on the entire Westside. First, as bait, I want the bitch that had Big-T on a hook. Her name is Stacy and she operates a business on the Westside and has twins. If we catch her and kill her then this will flush him out. Here is a picture of her," Ricky said while passing out several photos to the crew.

"She pretty as hell, this should be fun," a short crew member spoke.

"Don't fucking underestimate no-one, especially this bitch!!!" Ricky yelled.

"These dudes are clever. Trust us, do not play around y'all," Tik reminded.

After giving the orders Ricky ended the meeting reminding everyone that in a few days that they would be headed to the city. Once he phoned Jeff to inform him to prepare for the hit squad; things would be ready. Jeff had accepted his role and days later the gangsters flew into Metro Airport headed for the eastside of Detroit.

Welcomed with fake I.D.'s, cars, money, and a hideaway that only a few knew about, they were ready for war. After a good night's sleep, they were briefed with new details about their targets and instructed to engage in battle.

Later that night they visited "The Sting Topless Bar" on the Westside of Detroit. Upon arriving they had made plans to walk in and cause trouble to send a message. To Jeff the good thing about having outsiders do the dirty work was that they could disappear afterwards. Pulling up to the hot spot everyone placed masks over their faces to hide their identity. Loading up the stolen weapons, all six exited the cars leaving Jeff behind to observe the event. Walking up to the front door a tall husky security guard greeted them and tried to shake them down. Quickly, Vaughn pulled out his 9mm and fired two shots into his stomach causing him to fall down. Jumping over his body they all rushed into the bar guns blazing; unnoticed due to the live entertainment from the topless dancers, the gunmen took direct aim.

Multiple shots ranged out as chaos erupted throughout the midsize bar. People were falling down, getting trampled on while trying to escape from the madness. Bullets tore through the flesh of many men and women alike, destroying the bars interior. Standing by the door one of the hit squad members fired a 12-gauge shotgun into the crowd hitting several people. Blood filled the floors and tables as if a massacre had occurred.

By the time the shooting stopped; 7 victims laid dead, while several others were seriously wounded. No one knew what happened or why it happened; the hit squad exited the bar and fled the scene.

Rushing back to the eastside down 8mile Road, they observed police cars and ambulances coming to the late rescue. At the crime scene police asked surviving witnesses details about the shootings as the Detectives arrived late.

"This shit is a mess" Detective Ross said.

"Yeah, looks like we got our work cut out for us tonight," Detective Freeman added.

As they stepped out the newly purchased Mark 8 Lincoln; they began to work fast. "Officers, take statements from all of the witnesses then turn them loose. We need to clear this shit up so C.S.I. and the coroners can do their jobs," Detective Ross demanded.

"You two give me the details of this here," Detective Freeman suggested.

"We'll sir it seems like several men entered the bar and shot everything moving. They started with the guard at the front door then extended their mission inside. All we have is 6 different gun casings and 7 dead with over 20 injured" the short bald officer explained.

"Did anybody give a motive or get a look at the perps?" Detective Ross asked.

"No sir, we were told that each one wore a colored mask that only showed their eyes," the officer replied.

"Shit, okay. Thanks a lot. Take the reports and statements and I'll catch you later," Detective Ross ordered.

Over the next few hours the detectives would canvas the area searching for clues to their case. It had been a few years since they had a case like this to figure out with very little evidence to go off of.

"O.K. I'll check out a few of my neighborhood connects to see if I can turn over a few rocks. Then I'll catch you tomorrow at the office," Detective Ross said after a brief conversation.

"Cool, I'll finish up here and do the same. Catch ya in the morning," Detective Freeman ended while putting out his cigarette.

On the other side of town, Jeff relayed the good news to Ricky about how they terrorized Rondo's hangout. Moments later Ricky watched the news on CNN in Miami as he gave the word to hit Stacy next.

Once Rondo had got the word from the news about the blood bath at the bar Doc and he laid low from that location not knowing that the hit was intended for them.

Meanwhile, at home, Stacy prepared for a long day at the office. It had been a few days since her and Tee-Tee heard about the bar shooting on the news. So, after realizing that the beef Rondo set off was close to home she decided to take several days off work. Staying at home was not an option and hiding out was even worse.

Stacy had her CPL license and was prepared for anything. Heading off to her place of business she was confident that today would be a good day. Upon arriving at the office Stacy parked in her CEO parking space next to the front door. Everyone at her business was excited to see her feeling better and looking good.

"Hello Ms. Moore," they all greeted.

"Hello everyone, it's good to be back, now let's get back to work," she joked.

Stacy sat in her office catching up on all the inventory and back orders that were neglected. Making calls to clients and occasionally calling Tee-Tee to gossip, she finally felt at ease. This was her sanctuary away from home and with the children in good care she relaxed.

Throughout the 10-hour shift Stacy had caught up with all the work she left behind. It was now time to go home to the children that she missed while working extra hours.

Locking up their stations, her employees wandered around the huge store saying their good-nights. Stacy was the last to leave as she set the alarm and headed toward her car. Outside the gallery two of the hit squad members waited inside the tan mini-van armed. Unaware Stacy walked to her car disarming the alarm system.

As she reached for the door handle the men jumped out the van and rushed towards her with guns drawn.

"Bitch, don't say a word!!!" the tall dude yelled.

"Oh my God!!! What I do-what I do?" Stacy asked scared to death.

"It don't matter now, let's go" the tall dude demanded.

While the hit squad had orders to shoot on sight from Ricky, these two had a plan of their own. While she begged for her life one of the masked men ran to grab the van. Approaching fast he slid the van door open and jumped out with the engine still running.

"Please don't kill me! Please don't kill me! I have kids!" Stacy cried.

"Shut up bitch and get the fuck in the van!!!" The gunmen demanded loudly.

Shoving her into the van they began to drive off while the heavy-set dude blind folded Stacy. In the back of the van the first man sized her up.

"I told you she was a pretty motherfucker," he shouted to the driver.

"Yeah, let's find a spot to fuck this hoe, then we'll kill her," the heavy dude suggested.

Driving several miles away from the gallery, the tall mask gunman planned to sexual assault her by playing with her pussy. As he held her hands together with one hand, he used the other to molest her. This gave Stacy who was not searched, an opportunity to slither loose and grab the hidden 380 caliber pistol in her lower back. Already off safety she allowed him to think that she wasn't resisting by opening her legs to be fingered.

"Yeah, act right baby, this will be ya last time getting some good dick," the tall gunmen said.

"Aye, we bout to park behind Sanders restaurant on Fenkell, cool?" the driver asked.

"Let's get it, hurry up nigga this hoe ready!" the tall gunmen shouted.

Seconds later they pulled back into the back parking lot of Sanders BBQ which was closed at the time. Stacy knew that if they found the gun on her that it would be over quickly. So instead she took her chance while they were thinking with their dicks. With his hands still in her panties and her one hand loose she grabbed the gun and fired.

Out of fear and blind folded with a large bag and tied with rope, Stacy aimed for the body of her molester hitting him in the stomach and groin area. Snatching off the bag as he dropped his gun, she fired shots at the driver before he could reach for his gun in the passenger seat. Out of panic, he froze up as a random bullet penetrated his skull.

Moments after Stacy looked at the wounded tall gunmen and screamed, "Why the hell would you do this to me? Why?" she yelled.

Running out of breath and life he couldn't speak at all.

"Ahhhhh, I hate you!" Stacy yelled as she fired several more shots into his frame, killing him instantly.

While the two men lay dead Stacy rushed out the van and ran to a pay phone to call Tee-Tee to help her.

Twenty minutes later she arrived and took Stacy home as they cried and called Rondo…

Chapter Six

At the police headquarters, detectives Ross and Freeman sat behind their desk conversing about their caseloads. In the middle of their conversation Detective Ross got a mysterious phone call.

"Homicide this is Detective Ross. May I help you?" he answered. He listened as an anonymous caller calls in to give a tip about the recent shooting. He quickly took down the information then relayed it to Detective Freeman.

"Hey, got something partner," Detective Ross said.

"Oh yeah, lay it on me," Detective Freeman said.

"I got this call from some lady telling me that all the senseless killings are due to that old case we had a few years back," Detective Ross stated.

"What case?" Freeman asked.

"You know, Stacy Moore and the two lovers ordeal. I guess both sides are beefing over revenge of some sort" Detective Ross stated calmly.

"Hmmm a Westside, Eastside to Miami quarrel huh? Let's check a few things out. Grab me a profile chart on all the crime families and contact Gang Squad for further Intel. We should be able to come up with a list of affiliates and maybe get the F.B.I. involved," Detective Freeman demanded.

"Gotcha, give me a few days until then we'll just play the field," Detective Ross suggested.

A few days after the kidnap attempt on Stacy, she sat at home uneasy talking to Rondo. "See what the hell you started? These niggas are trying to kill me!" She shouted.

"Cool down shorty, you alright. Nine times out of ten Ricky was gone try to kill you out of loyalty for his boy anyhow. The streets are talking and if they seem tender dick over some pussy then their hustle would disappear," Rondo explained.

So now what Rondo? I killed two niggas and was almost raped and killed boy! I got kids!" she yelled again.

"I know I'm placing two men on you 24/7 and I'm adding 4 undercover men into the store for extra safety," he explained again.

"Rondo you need to quit this stupid shit for your ass gets killed. Is that what you want? Stacy asked.

"I want my boy back and since that can't happen then fuck everybody," he said walking out the house angry.

Stacy failed to follow after him and felt his pain deep down inside. They were all hurting over her actions and they both had the scars and wounds to remind them. She figured that she'd let him calm down and just use the extra bodies around her to be safe.

Back on the Eastside, Jeff thought about calling Ricky to tell him about the fuck up. He had two dead bodies on his hands and a more alert than ever Stacy. Fucking up was something that Ricky didn't tolerate and to call with bad news wasn't ever good. Picking up the cell he dialed the secure line that Ricky kept available.

"Talk to me," Ricky answered drowsy.

"Hey fam just called to give you the 411 on shit," Jeff spoke.

"Lay it on me quickly," he said.

Over the next few minutes Jeff explained the latest situation and outcome.

"What the fuck did I tell you motherfuckers?" I specifically said don't underestimate these people. We are at war in a different city and niggas down there playing! I'm glad them dumb motherfuckers got killed trying to rape that bitch!" Ricky yelled through the phone.

"Yeah, I told them to kill on sig—"Jeff tried to explain before he was interrupted.

"Shut up! You're the leader down there, but yet you act like you're not in control. The six of you better get in order or I'll put all of your heads on EBay to the highest bidder. Make sure Tik is picked up tomorrow to help run shit!" Ricky said before hanging up and throwing the cell in the fish tank.

Sitting back on his couch nursing the wounds from the gunshots, Ricky thought to himself, 'Man things getting crazy in the 'D' it might be time to pull out and relocate. Only if Terrance was here to help guide a nigga, damn I miss you boy,' he thought as he fell asleep...

Chapter Seven

Inside the real estate office that Rondo ran for Joey's dad, he sat with Mr. Anderson. As they discussed the legal side of things he also inquired about the streets.

"Well Mr. Anderson things on the streets have been kind of messy," Rondo said.

"No shit, listen to me really good, little man. I make 3-million a year from moving my product through the Fenkell Boyz. I've been the leader and original gangster since the birth of this crew. I lost my son to love not the streets. The beef you caused is not good for business," Mr. Anderson responded smoking a Rocky Patel Cigar.

"Sir, if we don't send a message then people will think we soft and run over us," Rondo stated politely.

"Being soft doesn't make you a coward, it makes you a thinker. People spend money to get ahead and profit. They don't care if you're soft or hard it's all about your business ethics. Showing honor to my son is great, but bringing heat to my doorstep and grandchildren is not. Since you started this in good faith I'll expect you to end it in the same manner. Get rid of that nigga now and let's get back to what we do----get money," Mr. A said standing up to exit.

"O.K. boss, I'm on it a.s.a.p." Rondo agreed.

Once the boss left the office Rondo called a meeting at the club house in Dearborn. Several of the elite members from the Fenkell Boys showed up to accept their orders. At the head of the long lavish oak wood table

sat Rondo.

"O.K. listen up everyone, it's time to step up our

art of war tactics. These nigga's been killing and fucking

up our clientele and name. Now, since they want to bring

it to our turf it's time that we took it to theirs," Rondo

spoke seriously.

"What ya got in mind buddy?" Doc asked.

"I'm taking four of you with me to take out this

nigga, Ricky," Rondo spoke again.

Everyone in the room looked on with confusion;

and a little skeptical.

"How this gone work Ron-Ron?" one member

asked.

"Easily, I got the info on his location, main chic

and family. We gone grab his son and bring him to

Detroit to negotiate his life for his. Trying to get a regular

hit on Ricky is impossible being that the Zoe Pound

Squad keeps him protected and after the hit was missed on him in the city; his security had been upgraded," Rondo spoke.

"Do we have anybody on the inside?" another dude asked.

"Of course, I had several people tail Ricky over the last few weeks. Plus, Doc and I know Miami like the city so he'll be going along to keep control," Rondo stated.

"O.K. ya got it! Everybody grab their I.D.'s and load up, we out in the morning to handle business," Doc ordered.

Once Doc and Rondo were alone they talked briefly about the new mission. "Damn fam this is a gutsy move ya did," Doc said calmly.

"It's got to be done in order to restore our control in the market," Rondo stated.

"Alright let's do it," Doc said.

"I'll have the guns and personal guide meet you in a few days at Club Star in Carol City," Rondo explained.

After talking they separated until the final days of Ricky appearance.

As the days turned into nights, time came for the transition to Miami to come into fruition. Doc and three other Fenkell Boyz members headed to Miami to meet up with 'Destiny,' their contact. The drive took 22 hours to complete so upon arriving they were all exhausted. Pulling into the hideout on the Southside of Little Haiti, they received their Intel before resting.

Inside the small house the next morning Doc awoke to find Destiny lying next to him. "Good morning gangsta," she spoke smiling.

"You real sneaky, I see," Doc responded.

"Well, today will be a busy day. I have the van out back and will take you to all the locations Rondo suggested. He told me to have you back in the city within

48 hours, so you must move fast. In those boxes are several weapons of your choice. We have M-16, AR-15, Sk's and multiple handguns. Inform your crew members to be precise and accurate, these guys in Little Haiti don't fuck around," she explained seriously.

"Cool, let's ride out. Alright y'all nigga's lay low until we ready to rock," Doc shouted to the crew before leaving.

They headed out to survey the area, after a while they noticed that Ricky was in hiding at a secret location. There was no sign of him at the house or his Exotic Car Business that he owned. After driving for a few hours Doc relayed the bad news to Rondo.

"Fam, this cat ain't around," Doc spoke.

"What ya mean? That's his home town," Rondo replied.

"Yeah, but Destiny took me everywhere and there is no sign of him at all. He's not throwing any parties or making any cameos around town," Doc explained.

"Damn, Destiny the truth at what she do. If she can't find him then we're fucked on this one," Rondo said.

"So what should we do? Just cause chaos like them?" Doc suggested.

In the middle of their conversation Destiny stopped to show Doc Ricky's little brother's house outside of Dade County. While still on the phone with Rondo they observed Ricky's 23-year old brother playing b-ball with Ricky's son.

"Fam check this out, we at dog crib and Destiny told me that this is his son and brother out here," Doc relayed.

"Word, well since he took something close to me, we'll take something closer to him," Rondo stated.

"What up doe?" Doc asked.

"Tell ya what, lil bro. Grab lil man and hit the e-way back home by all means. I think I know how to flush this dude out, Holla." Rondo ordered as he hung up the cell.

"Alright, let's get back to the crib so we can formulate a plan for this task," Doc told Destiny.

Twenty minutes later they were back at the house preparing to lay out the new details. Once everyone got on the same page they strapped up with weapons and headed out on their mission.

Thanking Destiny for all the support she gave, Doc handed her an envelope containing 10 thousand dollars cash. Keeping the van as a mobile station Doc and the crew proceeded to grab the young boy. Piled up in a van along with duct tape, rope, and ski masks things seemed logical.

At the location Ricky's brother remained outside in the front yard of the suburb areas. Inside the gated home the little boy played alone with several body guards around. The crew counted 6 armed men in the front and backyard. Waiting for the right moment to catch them off guard to avoid gunplay; the crew sat for approximately an hour trying to wait it out or hoping that the brother and boy left the home.

Since it was almost dark outside Doc decided to attack and grab the boy.

"Listen, grab the heat and you two come with me while you grab the boy and get back to the van," Doc ordered.

Placing the ski masks over their face and loading up the assault rifles, it was time to move. Unnoticed they jumped out the van parked a half block down. Hiding behind the trees and brush that secluded the home, they took aim at the security. They knew that time was of the essence and had to use the dark to their advantage. Once everyone was in position Doc gave the go ahead to engage in shooting the guards.

As the crew sniped several guards and held the rest at bay firing into the darkness. The short quick Fenkell Boy member they call 'Speedy' approached the gate as bullets flew.

Unaware of what was going on; Ricky's brother grabbed his nephew and ran for the bunker on the side of the mini mansion. As they tried to run, Speedy gave chase with his 40 caliber in hand; with shots being fired and 5 of the 6 guards lying dead or wounded.

Doc entered the gate and ran the opposite direction of the chase while the others checked for survivors.

Catching up to the victims Speedy commanded them to stop. Ricky's brother did as he was told as he held on to his nephew for dear life. Suddenly out of the corner of Speedy's eye he saw one of the guards approaching fast. Before he could react, the last thing he heard was

BANG!!!

The guard shot Speedy in the head leaving him for dead. Seconds later while running toward the baby and brother Doc heard a shot; running faster toward the sound he saw the body of Speedy dropping to the ground and the victims getting away.

Taking aim, he began shooting rapidly at them from 25feet. Instantly the guard dropped from a single bullet to the rear skull. Ricky's brother slowed down while holding the 6-year old and being hit in the knee cap.

As he fell in the driveway Doc grabbed the young boy and called for the crew. Lying on the pavement the victim pleaded for help and his life. "Please don't shoot, please!!! Ricky brother yelled.

"Too late nigga, an eye for an eye and a tooth for a tooth!" Doc spoke before pulling the trigger and landed a single shot that ended his existence.

The rest of the squad rushed to the van with Ricky's son as the sounds of police sirens got closer. In the van, they ducted taped and tied the boy's hands together. Covering his face with a mask was too bold so they placed a sweat band across the eyes. It was now time to head back home with a calm, but worried little boy.

The drive would be easy as they dumped the weapons and costumes in the city garbage bins. On the way home, Doc called Rondo to let him know that things were cool.

After the phone call Rondo had felt like he accomplished a major blow in the war. As soon as he had the boy, he would phone Ricky and negotiate his life for his son's.

A day and a half later the crew pulled into Rondo's secret location in Novi, Michigan. He wanted to keep the boy safe from wandering neighbors and police. In due time, he would call Ricky to talk to him about paying a ransom. He figured that since he'll be in a jam, why not hurt his heart and pockets before killing him.

Placing the youngster in the back room, they untied him and allowed him to eat. Sitting in the small room with a T.V., video games, and a bed, the little boy started to cry.

Doc and Rondo had a little remorse as the tears rolled down his cheeks as he cried for his family.

"Man, lock the door from the outside and check on lil dude every 30minutes," Rondo told his captain.

"What about letting him use the bathroom?" the captain asked. "Motherfucker, if you let a 6-year old escape from this bitch then you need to be shot dead. Do the fucking job!" Doc yelled.

As they prepared to head to a different location to call Ricky from a pay phone; Rondo gave orders to burn the van and clothes then lay low until they returned.

Leaving Novi, Rondo and Doc jumped into his Red Viper Car and headed to Pontiac, Michigan to make the call. They realized that if the call was made from a cell phone then it could be tracked by the phone towers. Calling from another city would throw off any investigation that secretly waited.

Pulling into a CVS parking lot, Rondo called the number that Destiny slid to Doc. "Heeeeellllllooooo there gangsta," Rondo spoke laughing.

"Who the hell is this?" Ricky answered angrily.

"This ya worse nightmare nigga, so shut up and listen!" Rondo demanded.

"Talk nigga!!!" Ricky shouted.

"So much aggression! Now, dig this. Never contact the police or I'll be forced to act worse. As you know we got your seed from up under your untouchable arms. He's

safe for now, but won't be if you don't bring me 1-million

cash and exchange your life for his," Rondo spoke.

"Don't hurt my boy, man! You already killed my

fucking brother nigga," Ricky responded.

"That was a small price to pay for the life of Kim

and the attempt on mine. I don't blame you for the death

of Joey, but your reaction was premature," Rondo spoke

again.

"Come on man, the hit wasn't for you," Ricky

explained before being cut off.

"Well, unfortunately I was there and I almost

didn't make it. So, in a few days I'll call you with the

instructions about the drop off and pick up, holla," Rondo

stated as he quickly hung up.

On the other end of the phone Ricky was nervous

and confused. His baby mother was in a rage over their

son and threatened to call the police. After a few hours of

yelling and fighting she was calmed down and led to a safe house.

Shortly after, Ricky called Tik and Jeff to have them find the location of his son quietly. Deep down inside his heart he knew that things had gotten out of hand, but to have involved his son was too much. So, over the next few days Ricky would strive to plan a miracle to regain his only son and spare his life as well…

Chapter Eight

Meanwhile, back in Canton, Stacy and Tee-Tee prepared to have a girl's night out. It had been a while since the pair enjoyed a little freedom and they both needed it. Unaware of the ongoing beef and kidnapping they decided to grab a bite to eat.

"Damn, girl you look nice," Tee-Tee joked getting into the car.

"Yeah, I clean up nice girl. You looking like you single, too. You mean to tell me that Rome crazy ass let you out like that?" Stacy joked back.

"Shit, his ass in Atlanta doing a show, so I'm letting my hair down respectfully," Tee-Tee replied.

"O.K., I thought it would be nice to go eat at 'Pizza Papalis' Downtown since my mom got the kids until 2am," Stacy suggested.

"It's cool with me, I love their deep-dish shrimp pizza anyway," again Tee-Tee stated while rolling a blunt.

Dressed in summer gear the women valet parked at the restaurant ready to enjoy their evening. Once greeted by the host they were sat in the middle of the pizzeria connected to the casino. Every eye in the place was glued to their frames as their silky hair blew in the cool breeze from the A.C.

"Damn, this place is packed as hell for a Friday," Tee-Tee said. "Aint it though" responded Stacy. After ordering their meal and drinks the two sat and observed the room as they talked about life. Suddenly, Tee-Tee noticed a table full of guys sitting in the back close to their table.

"Cee-Cee, look at all those niggas over there at the back table," Tee said.

"Damn, they deep as hell and they all wearing blue," Stacy responded.

"The tall one got his eyes locked on you from a distance," Tee-Tee laughed.

"Shut up girl, he ain't thinking about me," Stacy replied.

"Oh shit, he's coming over," Tee-Tee whispered.

In the middle of their conversation the tall gentlemen approached them in a greeting manner. "Hello sexy my name is Damon, can I have a second of your precious time?" he asked calmly.

Stacy had watched him stroll across the room as she took in his description. He stood 6-foot, 9inches, 230 lbs., caramel skin, with muscles, and a perfect set of teeth. He looked like a healthy basketball player with the jewels to match. Reaching out her hand to shake his, she spoke softly. "My name is Stacy. Nice to meet you Damon," she replied.

"May I have a seat?" he asked.

"Sure, join us. This is my best friend, Tee-Tee," she introduced politely. They both greeted with a smile and brief hello. Seconds later, after a quick conversation, the waiters arrived with their meal. Not wanting to be rude Damon excused himself until after the meal was completed.

"Well Stacy it's been a pleasure meeting you and truthfully I don't want to leave, but I respect that you must eat. However, I and a few of my closest comrades will be visiting the casino to engage in a little sport and play. You and Tee-Tee, is it? You're both welcome to join us for a good time with no strings attached. Plus, this will allow us a little more time to talk," he spoke convincingly.

Stacy thought for a minute then turned to talk to Tee-Tee. "What you think sis?" she asked.

"They seem cool and it is an open environment that's safe. Plus, we were going there next, so why not?" Tee-Tee spoke.

"O.K. cool Mr. Damon, we'll except the invite and meet y'all there by the Blackjack tables," Stacy said.

"Cool, I'll let my body guard know and I'll also let everyone know that your cute friend is married," he joked as he smiled.

Standing up about to leave the ladies, Stacy stopped him to ask a few questions. "Hey, how old are you and where are you from Damon?" She questioned.

"I'm 38 and born and raised in Chicago," he responded.

"I knew you weren't from the city," Tee-Tee said jokingly.

"How could you tell?" he asked her.

"Your swagger and accent is different. What set y'all claiming?" Tee-Tee asked being that she learned a lot from Rome about the gang life.

"I'm a 2nd ranked Gangster Disciple under the guidance of Larry Hoover and the Six. Plenty much boss ladies," he stated.

"Never too much," Tee-Tee said and smiled.

After the exchange of words Damon returned to his table to inform the crew of the changes.

"Girl, how you know about that stuff and what does it mean?" Stacy asked curiously.

"Rome been banging since birth girl and he's a G.D. That dude is highly ranked and he call the shots for over 85-percent of the million plus gang. All that I can say is that he's connected and powerful," Tee-Tee explained.

Stacy listened and took notes not feeling threatened or amazed with his status. She was quite used to being around power from Joey and money wasn't an object because she was worth a few million herself.

Shortly after their meal was finished, the two prepared to do a little gambling while enjoying their night out. Walking through the upper level of the restaurant they made their way to the connecting casino. Approaching the blackjack tables, they could see Damon and several members waiting on them.

"Glad you kept ya word, sexy. Here have a seat and don't mind the dudes in blue, they're only here to protect you," Damon explained.

In front of the ladies the dealer slid 25Grand in chips a piece, and then began to deal the cards.

"Wow, all this for me already? Baby, I got my own money," Stacy said.

"So do I. Let's just call this our first date of many and the next time will be on you," Damon joked.

"You already know it's a part two, huh?" Stacy asked.

"Of course, you look like the type of woman that knows what is best for you," he smiled and spoke.

"You know that's right! Let's gamble," Stacy said with grin.

Over the next 5 hours the crew and the ladies visited multiple tables as they shot dice and played poker. The night was perfect and Stacy was enjoying the company of her new friend. At 2am time was getting late and it was time to exit the casino. Tee-Tee was also tired and they both had won a little over six grand.

Walking to the cash out counter Stacy repaid the fifty Grand back to Damon and kept the profits. He was amazed at the level of class she displayed as he volunteered to walk them to their car.

On the way, they talked and laughed as Tee-Tee witnessed her friend happy for the first time in a while.

Exchanging numbers Damon let her know that he would be leaving town in a few hours, but would return in a week. They promised to link up on a more solid, but quiet bases when he returned.

On the way, home the women talked about the evenings events. "I see you had a good time," Tee-Tee spoke lazy.

"Yeah, it was nice and Damon made a good impression with his sexy ass," Stacy responded.

"I agree sis, hopefully you'll see him again and maybe y'all might hit it off?" Tee-Tee said.

"Let's just let nature take its' course. He seemed cool, but I'm not ready to date again" Stacy said.

"Listen, life goes on, Stacy. And the only way to get over your past is to live for the future. Trust me let your heart lead the way and the rest will follow. Joey is gone and it's up to you to move on," Tee-Tee said.

"You're right Tee, but its hard cause of the kids. I'm going to work on opening up," she replied flicking her wrist like Wendy Williams.

Pulling up to Tee-Tee's house they said their good-nights and Stacy headed home with thoughts of Damon flashing through her mind.

The next few days Stacy worked and enjoyed time with the kids and Ms. Moore. Spending quality time with her family was always a relaxing event. Eventually, she would call Tee-Tee to check on her, but she would always be busy with Rome.

Being a wife was something Stacy yearned for and sought after ever since Joey came into her life. To fill the void would take a lot of healing and maturity. Once she realized that everyone would not be Joey or meet the standards of him, and then the healing process would begin.

On Saturday, the following weekend while Stacy watched the kids pay in the yard. Her cell phone rang with a unique number and area code.

"Hello this is Stacy" she answered in her professional voice.

"How you doing? This is Damon, remember me?" Damon asked.

"Oh you, huh? I thought I paid my debt off? When will my debt be cleared?" she joked back.

"50years from now, only cause I can get use to you," he said.

"Oh yeah, that's a major statement," she said.

"Everything I do is major sweetie," he said.

"Well that's good playa, but I'll have to take you up on our second date at a later time," Stacy spoke kindly.

"Why wait, is there a problem with me?" he asked.

"Oh no, it's just that you caught me off guard today. I'm a mother of 5-year old twins and my baby sitter is out today," she explained.

"I understand that, but that alone shouldn't stop us from seeing each other," Damon said.

"Oh yeah?" she smiled on the phone.

"Oh yeah, girl," he replied.

"Tell ya what, I don't ever go against my principles on dating. But my girl just told to let my old ways go and try to be spontaneous. So, how about you come to my house and we can kick it for a while?" she suggested.

"I would like that very much, sexy. I know that you don't let dudes come to your crib or be around your children," Damon said.

"How you know that?" she asked.

"Your personality and swagger, you seem like a loner or person who has been hurt before. You're beautiful, smart, and single, this is rare," Damon explained.

"You better believe it," she joked surprised.

"I'll come out of my comfort zone as well and come by myself. Guess the both of us are letting our guard down and learning to trust. What's the directions?" he asked.

After several minutes of talking Stacy gave him the directions with plans to see him in an hour. She had never stepped outside of her comfort zone like this before. However, listening to Tee-Tee and feeling that this dude was older and an outsider, she took a chance.

An hour later, Damon pulled up in an all Blue Rolls Royce Ghost. Starring out the window Stacy observed him park in the horseshoe shape driveway. Walking up to the door she noticed his muscles through the Gucci Jogging suit and tank top he sported.

"Hello stranger, welcome to my humble headquarters," she greeted opening the door.

"Hello back to you sexy, you look wonderful and relaxed," he stated.

Stacy had sported a tennis skirt, house shoes and a matching tank top. "Thank you, please come in and we can chill on the back porch," she suggested.

The pair entered the large patio to engage in conversation and to keep a watchful eye on the children. Stacy explained to the kids that Damon was a friend and they enjoyed playing with him. Watching them interact with a dude was something new to her. The only other male that had been around was Rondo, their God dad.

Damon was a pleasure to be around and very respectful toward the children. The two had drunk a few glasses of white wine as they spoke on every level. He explained to her his life style, upbringing and future goals as she covered her entire past. To Stacy it felt odd speaking about her being a cheater, but it also made her look honest. To her surprise Damon had sincerely understood her past and accepted all that he took in. The mood was mild, and jazz played on the mini outside system, strangely the doorbell sounded.

"Don't worry Dee, I'm not expecting anyone," she noted.

"Is that a good thing or what?" he joked taking his gun off safety. In his mind, he had a vision of the story that she just explained about the murder suicide. So, just to be on the safe side he wanted to be alert since this was not something that he did often.

On her way to the door, Stacy saw Rondo's Red Viper parked in the driveway. "Oh my God, shit I forgot that he was coming over to see the kids today," she thought unconsciously. Quickly she yelled to Damon not to worry and to tell him it was the kids God Daddy at the door.

"What up doe Cee-Cee?" Rondo spoke.

"Shit, boy, you always late. I forgot you were coming over," she responded.

"Oh yeah, where the babies at and who dude out front?" he asked looking around the house.

"Dang, you nosey boy!!! Yes, I have company so don't start tripping," she said in a low voice. Rondo followed her to the back patio to call for the kids. Damon sat on the lounge chair awaiting their arrival. "Rondo this is my friend Damon from the Chi and Damon this is my kids God Daddy, Rondo," she explained as she introduced them.

"What up doe fam?" Rondo greeted with a handshake.

"Nice to meet you. I've heard nothing, but good things about you," Damon stated.

"That's good. I'mma let y'all chill while I check on the twins," Rondo said looking spooked.

During the next thirty minutes Damon and Stacy continued to talk as she explained more about her life. In the midst of their conversation Rondo came back into the house upset as he got her attention.

"Yo, let me holla at you, Cee," Rondo demanded.

"Boy, calm down. Here I come," she responded while giving the '1-second sign' to Damon.

In the living room Rondo faced off with Stacy in a heated conversation about her actions. "Why this nigga out here in my boy crib?" Rondo asked.

"First of all boy, I'm grown and this is my motherfucking house! What I do or do it with is my business," she responded waving her hands.

"Fuck that Stacy! I'm out here beefing with niggas over a decision you made, while you getting lovely-dovey with this dude," Rondo stated.

"Listen boy, my life doesn't revolve around your street justice. You're doing that shit to satisfy your own pride and greed. Joey would want me to be happy…"

She tried to finish, but Rondo stormed out the door. "Fuck it I'm out! Stupid ass," he said rushing to the car.

Stacy was upset as she strolled back into the patio to chat with Damon. After a few minutes of discussion Damon gave his opinion of the situation. "Dig sexy, I respect what Rondo is doing for you and his crew. Truthfully, I support his actions cause he a street nigga living by the code. I'm familiar with the beef and I know Mr. A through a mutual associate. I never met Joey, but heard a little about him. My crew dealt with both sides of the beef only because we supply the zones with 85-percent of their product," he explained.

"So why didn't you tell me this before? Did you know who I was when we met?" Stacy asked suspiciously.

"Of course not, I was attracted to your beauty the second we locked eyes. I only listened to your story to identify any lies. Once you started talking, I put two and two together along with the unknown facts from the streets. At that point, I realized that you were the woman they call 'Ms. Killer Pussy.'" Damon explained standing up to leave.

"Damn, I'm lost for words," she stated.

"Please don't be, I enjoyed your company and would love to see you again before I leave. Tell the children I said good-bye and maybe we could plan a trip to the zoo this weekend," he said smiling.

"So, my past doesn't scare you?" She asked.

"I don't scare easy sexy, until next time," he joked heading for the door.

Watching him walk away, she stood in the doorway thinking about how small the world is and how her past affects her future...

Chapter Nine

The next day after Rondo left Stacy's home. He and Doc prepared to meet Ricky on their terms and grounds. Thankfully, Ricky was willing to pay the ransom and exchange his life for his son's.

After carefully putting a G.P.S locator in the money and securing a full proof getaway plan, he was finally ready. Driving to Detroit he focused on the entire layout as he convinced his son's mother not to panic.

In the city Rondo set Doc up at the drop off spot located on the Westside near Bright 'Mo. In another location he had Rick's son tied to a chair in an abandon house with two crew members. Rondo had arranged for Ricky to drop the money off to Doc and then the boy would be dropped off immediately. Once the son arrived Doc would take Ricky at gunpoint to the street location, while Ricky's team got the boy.

On the way to the drop off point Ricky hatched his plan in motion to regain control of the situation. Pulling up to the large building on Lasher Rd. Ricky observed Doc sitting in a U.P.S. van. He was wearing a brown outfit with dreads along with two other huge gunmen. Fearing for his life Ricky jumped out unarmed and headed to hand the suitcase full of money over. As he walked toward the van his two body guards kept their A.K.'s aimed at the U.P.S. truck.

Suddenly, Doc's phone rang with a call from Rondo as Ricky's cell rang with a call from Detroit Detectives.

"Hello?" Doc answered.

"Get out of there! It's a set up! They got an Amber Alert out for the boy. Give him the address and bounce!" Rondo demanded before hanging up

"You fucked up! Ricky hand over the cash!!" Doc ordered angrily.

Ricky stood looking at his phone unaware of the news as he passed the suitcase over. Doc threw the address on the concrete and sped off before Ricky's crew could let off any shots or give chase.

Again, the phone rang as Ricky looked surprised that the money was gone and the plan had changed. "What!" he answered.

"This is Detective Ross from the Detroit Homicide Unit. We want to help you. Listen, your girl had us put an Amber Alert out on your son and called us for help," he explained quickly.

"No fucking way! This dumb bitch done got him killed! I don't need any help from any police!" he yelled.

At this time, his line beeped in with a call from Rondo. Briefly, before Rondo called Ricky he decided to call the man holding the child hostage.

"Hey boss," the young dude answered.

"Kill him quickly and exit to plan B," Rondo spoke in a rush.

Following orders, the young dude placed the revolver to the child's head and pulled the trigger.

Since Rondo had Ricky on the phone he explained the news. "You crossed me so now he's dead, pick him up at the address," Rondo said calmly as he hung up.

"No!!! Let's go!!!" Ricky yelled as he jumped into the car to find the address. 30 minutes later they pulled up to the vacant house on Dexter and Davidson. The house was surrounded by police as a neighbor called the shooting in anonymously.

"Hello, I'm Detective Ross and this is my partner Mr. Freeman," The older gentlemen greeted.

"Where is my fucking son?"

"Calm down sir, let us talk to you in private please," Detective Ross stated.

"Hell naw, let me see my boy," Ricky demanded with tears in his eyes.

While the detectives tried to calm down an irate father, the crime scene was sealed off. Seconds later the coroners came to take away the young frail body as Ricky went into shock.

"Sir let us help you! Who did this to your family?" Detective Ross asked.

"I'll send my family to view the body and have it flown to Miami. Please detectives stay out of my way, I mean it!" he said as he headed for the airport in anger.

"This shit is getting out of hand! We must gather more evidence on the Fenkell Boyz before we can bring a solid indictment," Detective Freeman suggested.

Several blocks away, the U.P.S. truck parked and watched the entire crime scene unfold. While in the vehicle, Doc overlooked the money that he never told Rondo he grabbed. He figured that it wouldn't matter as he greased the palms of the henchmen with him.

Doc reported to Rondo the presence of the nosey detectives and later headed to the airport to see Ricky off quietly.

Back in Canton, two days later, Stacy enjoys a deep conversation over the phone with Damon. It's been over a week since his visit, so they talked each night to get closer on building their bond. During a phone call with Stacy, Damon explained to her that he had recently had a business meeting with Mr. A. At the meeting Rondo was surprisingly present as a soldier as they came to the discussion about her. He politely informed them that unconsciously the two met and are becoming an item quickly. Then he went on to explain that out of respect he would like permission to continue this bond without conflict of interest. After deliberating for a few moments Mr. A agreed with the relationship and demanded that his grandchildren be respected. Mr. A had known Damon for several years through his father, another high ranked G.D. official.

Being that their business had now become solid as the G.D's took over as their head supplier. To everyone present this meant peace and prosperity for both families.

Damon had respected Rondo and wanted to reach out to him to try to end the rival with Ricky. Unable to do so if he tried, Damon's advice would of only fell on death ears, especially since the life of a child had been taken.

Moments after Stacy and Damon talked she joked about being a pawn in their game. So, to make her feel better he invited her and the kids to come to Chicago to visit the new city zoo. Excepting his offer, that Saturday they would meet again on his grounds. Spending time with him was something that she enjoyed and so did the twins. They had taken a liking to his soft side and the way he made their mom smile.

Since he now had the go ahead from Mr. A, the time he devoted to the family would be priceless. Once they arrived in Chicago, Damon would set them up in a Penthouse Suite Downtown. The Suite had 3 bedrooms and 2 bathrooms and a view of the entire inner city.

He would also allow Stacy to drive his 760 Series B.M.W. as a means of transportation. Everything needed to be perfect as he explained to the crew that security had no room for errors. He also made a secret attempt to introduce her to his mother Mrs. Green.

Awaiting their arrival was a sure adrenaline rush, but only patience could keep him calm. Falling in love with Stacy was something he didn't plan and hopefully it wasn't the wrong thing to do.

So, until Saturday, Damon laid back as he planned

to spend a few weeks with his new wifey...

Chapter Ten

Time had flown past in Detroit and it was now a year and a half since that whole situation with the child occured. The wind was mild and the temp was 86 degrees with plenty sunshine. Over the last several months things had calmed down in the streets. The beef had taken a turn for the best as the Detectives ran out of leads and received no cooperation from Ricky's family.

Rondo was still being supplied by Damon and Doc continued to be his right-hand man. Unfortunately, Rondo was still unaware of the money that Doc kept from the ransom.

Back in Canton, Stacy and the kids were still moving forward with life. Her relationship with Damon was slowly progressing as they declared to be a couple and the children had grown accustom to him being around and respected the relationship whole heartedly.

As the streets talked about the present killings, relationships, and up and coming bosses. Tee-Tee and Stacy listened and observed while the Motor City flip flopped.

The word in the underworld was that Rondo was King and being backed by the Chicago Syndicate. His main friend Doc had also come up on a lick for a million dollars and the Eastside crews wanted revenge for Tone's death. Everyone kept their eyes open, knowing that Ricky wouldn't just let his son's death slide. Since it had been a year and a half, the element of surprise was yet soon to come.

Ricky was in South Beach at the 4040 Club talking on his cell to Jeff. Jeff remained a loyal soldier as he distributed Ricky's product throughout the city. Ricky had informed Jeff that he'd be in the Detroit this weekend to meet with Damon.

Unaware of the connections Stacy or the Fenkell Boyz, he set up a meeting in Royal Oak, Michigan. The meeting would be based on creating a universal pipe line from Miami to Chicago to Detroit. Expressing to Jeff how important security had to be since it's been a while since the kidnapping and hit on his life.

Ricky surrounded himself with extra muscle and henchmen that held a certain bond with him. On the phone Jeff understood the urgency as he played his part in the matter.

Strategically preparing for a quick visit Ricky summoned his crew and demanded that Tik bring the G.P.S. tracker in case his money showed up.

Several days later Ricky arrived in Detroit via plane and headed to the meeting accompanied by his squad. On the other side of town Rondo sat at the office unaware of the secret visit. He had been feeling a little distance from Doc ever since he observed his new lifestyle and fortune. Rondo knew Doc was loyal and had access to making a lot of money being his wingman. However, the rumors and expensive spending traits always gave him a reason to have his radar up.

Doc had no idea that the word on the streets had gotten to Rondo. By him being caught up in his own world of lust and power he neglected to stay firm in his decisions. He would spend recklessly and a lot of times he would carry a hundred thousand in a small Gucci backpack that stayed stashed in his car trunk. Everybody in the hood nicknamed Doc, 'The Mayweather of Detroit'.

Meanwhile, an hour away in upper Royal Oak, Damon and Ricky sat at a large brick table. After several hours of negotiating the deal and format, it was approved. As the day headed into the mist of dawn a soldier of Ricky's whispered into his ear. "Excuse me sir," the soldier said.

"What is it?" Ricky responded aggressively.

"We have a hit on the GPS," he replied.

"Load up the car and van. We'll leave in a second. Don't lose the fucking signal!" he demanded.

Next, he politely turned to Damon who looked offended by the whispering and spoke, "Sorry about that. I gotta head to the city to handle some unfinished business. It's been a pleasure doing business with you as always and please tell the fam I send my blessings. I'll contact you once I'm back at home to arrange for the 1st shipment of many," Ricky said.

"Stay safe and prosper. Remember, make money not war," Damon reminded him. They both got up from the table and exited the large room to go their separate ways.

Outside in the parking lot Jeff sat inside the large Yukon Truck. "What up doe fam? I got the location of the money, but…" he was interrupted.

"But what? Round up several of the men and get that money back," he demanded calmly.

"Well it's kinda hard because on this screen it's showing that the money has been moving the last 4 hours," Jeff explained.

"What the fuck you mean?" Ricky asked.

"It's like the money is in his pocket or someone else has been giving the bills with the locator," he responded.

"Let's track this shit. Everyone load up and be prepared to kill on sight. I need my motherfucking money. Hopefully we'll catch Rondo ass at the same time. I'll follow in the car, let's go!" Ricky yelled.

Driving off Jeff lead the crew toward the moving dot on the keypad he held. Everyone was strapped with handguns and searching for the target.

"Got it, make a right on Oakman," Jeff said. Approaching a Dairy Queen, the dot alerted that this was the exact spot.

"We here, Ricky," Jeff chirped to let him know.

"It's probably inside here, or wait a minute," he paused as he stared into the crowded line.

"What's up Rick?" Tik asked while sitting in the driver seat.

"Aye I think that nigga right there is the same dude who I met in the UPS suit. Straight up, I remember those silly ass dreads," Ricky explained.

Doc was next in line to order and receive his blizzard that he craved. After smoking several blunts he decided to engage in a small frozen treat to ease his buzz. Walking back to his new Black Jaguar X.F. he noticed a few strange vehicles circling the area. Making a brief photo memory of the characters inside the cars, one dude stood out. Once inside the car he quickly grabbed the 40 caliber handgun out of the stash and slowly drove off.

Doc was unaware that Ricky and his team followed him easily due to the tracker located inside the money he stored in his trunk. Speeding toward the Davidson Freeway going west, he figured that the marijuana had him paranoid. Relaxed and driving to the sounds of his new Jezzy C.D., Doc noticed in the rear view several of the same vehicles on his tail. Quickly he placed a round in the chamber as he rolled the window down to catch a breeze.

Suddenly, the car that occupied Ricky and Tik sped past confirming the target as the G.P.S. beeped faster.

"That's the nigga, handle that!!!" Ricky chirped to the following gunmen.

As they passed by to position themselves in front of Doc's car, Doc looked up to glance into the passing car as he recalled the familiar face. "Oh shit! That's Ricky ass. It's a hit!" he thought out loud.

Too late, as the words exited his mouth the large Yukon truck pulled along the passenger side and started firing shots. Multiple shots hit the car on the freeway as Doc tried to shift through the traffic engaged in a shootout.

Swerving into the center lane with Tik blocking in front, Doc was hit in the rib and arm as he lost control of the steering wheel. The Jaguar slammed into the center lane divider which made the air bag pop out and knock Doc unconscious. Once he hit the wall the car stopped as the horn blew non-stop leaving no signs of life.

To be sure that the job was done Jeff drove past and ordered that several clips be emptied into the smashed car for reassurance. Next, the squad rushed to place Ricky on the first flight back home as he gave his final orders.

"Listen, y'all did well, but Rondo is still alive. Find him and finish this shit. Flush him out by burning down that bitch business he's protecting. I'll be in touch in a few days," Ricky spoke outside the airport.

Back at the crime scene, Detective Ross and Freeman oversaw another investigation. "This shit is getting to be a problem," Detective Ross said.

"Yeah, things were quiet for a while, but from the looks of it the action is back on," Detective Freeman responded.

"Sir, may we show you something?" the female officer asked.

Walking back to the smashed car they observed a backpack, "This is what we found in the trunk and we identified the victim as Donzell Ryan a Fenkell Boyz captain," she explained.

"Oh shit, that's gotta be at least a quarter million, and the victim had a gun in his hand, hmmm," Detective Freeman spoke.

"Could this be the case of the missing money? Maybe the gossip is true," Detective Ross added.

"Tag and bag all this shit and umm---hold up a second. What is this?" Detective Freeman asked while searching the bag full of money.

"Well sir, it looks like some sort of tracking device that you can get at a local spy shop or something," the small but cute officer suggested.

"That's it! That's it!" Detective Freeman said to his partner.

"RICKY!!!!" they both shouted out at the same time.

While the crime scene was taped off and the detectives began their questioning of a few witnesses, on another part of town several of Ricky's goons had succeeded at setting Stacy's place of business on fire.

In midday Stacy received a call from the local fire department explaining that her Art Gallery was overcome by flames. No one was injured but her entire inventory was destroyed. Luckily, her insurance company would cover most, but not all the losses and damages. Her heart dropped to her stomach as thoughts of the losses hit home. Suddenly the chief on the phone suggested that the fire was caused by an arsonist.

"We have found a few bomb devices in the debris, which gives us the inclination of an arsonist," the chief explained.

"What!!! Who would do something like this?" she questioned as she prepared to head out.

On her way to the shop Stacy contacted Damon who was enraged about the incident. Next, she phoned Rondo only to find out that Doc was killed several hours prior. "Oh my God Rondo, I'm sorry to hear that, what happened?" she asked curiously.

"Shit, somebody chased him on the e-way and got at him. They say he had big numbers in his trunk too," Rondo sadly replied.

"That's so sad. I know that was your boy, too. If you need somebody to talk to just stop by, ok? I'm about to check on the store," Stacy replied.

"Cool, this shit kinda strange if ya ask me. Doc gets killed then hours later your store is in flames. Plus, the fireman says it was arson. Be careful up there and once I help plan this funeral for Doc, I'll check into that too, catch ya later," Rondo said while recalling the events.

Seconds later Stacy pulled up to the burnt building to overlook the damage. To her surprise Damon stood to the side with his arms folded showing an angry demeanor. "Hey honey," she spoke.

"Sorry about this shit. Don't worry, you'll be up and back running within a few months," he spoke without a smile.

"Thanks Boo! I'm not worried, the insurance will cover most of it anyhow," she replied.

"You finish up here and I'll pick you up at 8:30pm at the house. I gotta handle some business," he demanded.

Damon was pissed off and wanted answers now. Nobody in their right mind would even think about harming anyone close to him. He immediately put out the word to his soldiers to find the people involved with this matter. "Listen, I need all of y'all to find the people involved in this shit. Somebody has to know something and I want answers. Spare no mercy and leave no stone unturned, got it?" Damon asked his crew with a serious face.

As the team set out to spread the word and seek information; Jeff got wind of the questioning ethics and quickly contacted Ricky to let him know that Damon was now involved with Stacy....

Chapter Eleven

Tonight would be a special and much needed night for Stacy. Spending time alone with Damon was something that she always enjoyed. Ms. Moore wasn't feeling good tonight so Tee-Tee agreed to look after the twins. Stacy was dressed in a Roksande Ilinic silk twill skirt and a silk top by Miu-Miu. She carried a Milly Samantha clutch velvet with 3inch DKNY leather sandals to match. After making up her face with light shadow and gloss, Stacy was as a cute as a baby doll.

Moments later Damon pulled up with no security in his new Cocaine colored Porshe with matching spinning wheels. He stepped out the car to open the Lambo style doors to allow her to enter. He casually sported a Gant Rugger cotton blazer with a pair of Folk-Suede and leather Armstrong shoes. On his face, he wore a pair of Raf Simons Aviator sunglasses with 5-karats of crushed diamonds in them.

"You ready to go I see, you look cute," he said smiling.

"Why thank you, and so do you boo," she replied blushing.

"Tonight, I'm taking you to 'Frenchies' in Sterling Heights, we have reservations," he explained driving.

"Oh yeah, I'm all for it. Let's do it," again she replied. On the drive to the restaurant they talked and enjoyed the sounds of Tyrese through the Bose Sound System. Pulling up to the five-star restaurant they entered and was seated near the live jazz band up front.

As their meals came, Damon reassured Stacy about their future. "Listen bae. Don't panic about the store because my boys are on top of the situation. I also talked to a couple of contractors who will get the job done within 6 months. Until then just enjoy your time off with the kids and me," Damon suggested.

"Owweeee, that's nice to hear Boo. I do need the rest and plus the twins are starting school this year also. Boy, they're growing up fast," she joked.

"O.K. let's toast to a new beginning and a wonderful night, despite the negative events that took place earlier," Damon suggested as he raised the champagne glass in a form of a toast.

"I'll drink to that," she replied as she did the same thing.

Several hours after their meal and desserts, the couple headed to Stacy's house to end the date.

"O.K. we here baby wake up," he said softly.

"Damn, I'm full and buzzed as hell," she said waking up.

"Let me walk you to the door sexy," he demanded.

"Oh, you not staying the night?" she asked angry but cute.

"I got another run to make honey, but I'll catch you for breakfast if ya like," he stated calmly.

Damon had never spent the night over Stacy's house due to the children and Ms. Moore. They had been dating for over 2 years and since the trip to Chicago, their sex life had been mild. She respected the fact that he had morals, but tonight she had none.

"Oh, you gone leave all this good shit alone and unprotected for another run?" she asked lifting up her skirt to show her pink thong.

Damon looked as she pulled off her skirt and top leaving nothing to the imagination, but her curvy body.

"You know you miss this good pussy. We need you," she said in her seductive voice opening the door.

"Shit, it's going to be a long night," he mumbled as he cut the car off and rushed inside. Stacy rushed to the bedroom as he followed stripping off his clothes. Lying on the bed he glanced at her beautiful body as he observed the scars on her neck and stomach. Slowly he began kissing and licking each mark to show her that he accepted every inch of her beautiful body. Biting on the neck while creeping downward to her sweet spot, he spread her legs wide open. Placing his fingers in the peace sign, he placed them on her wet pussy only to open her up wider. Attacking he pussy with a fury of tongue tricks, he sent her into another world. She moaned as her inner thighs ached from cumming repeatedly.

Once he was finished spending special time on her, she willingly returned the favor by pleasing him with lavish head. Up and down, side to side she bobbled like a snake hypnotizing its prey. Using her soft hands, she grabbed his waist and forced him deep inside her mouth until she slightly gagged. Damon was massive no doubt as Stacy enjoyed jacking his penis until he came all over her tongue.

Seconds later she took the lead and climbed onto the bed only to place a pillow under her stomach. Inching all the way up to the headboard she placed her forehead deeply into the large pillows. This allowed her ass to rise above waist high to Damon. From behind he observed her sweet juices flowing down her thighs as he calmly entered from the back.

After several minutes of lustful pumping and matching each other's heartbeats, he exploded inside her aggressively. Once they finished their love making session they fell asleep in the spoon position until morning.

The next morning Stacy was awakened by the sounds of her phones on the night stand. The number on the caller I.D. was unknown as she reached to answer it.

"Hello" she answered.

"Hi good morning is this Stacy Moore?" the strange professional voice spoke.

"Yes, it is. May I ask whose calling?" she replied.

"Of course, this is Doctor Amin from the Brownstown Hospital. I retrieved your number from your mother's personnel information sheet" he replied.

"My mother!!! Is she o.k., what's wrong?" she shouted as Damon woke up startled.

"She was brought to the hospital by ambulance last night. She has been suffering from chest pains over the last few weeks. My staff has run several tests on her and by the afternoon we shall have the results," the older Doctor spoke.

"Oh my God, please let her know that I'm on my way down immediately," she cried.

After hanging up the phone Stacy explained to Damon the current situation. Then as she got dressed she called Tee-Tee to have her bring the kids to the hospital a.s.a.p.

An hour later everyone arrived at the hospital anxious to know the results of Ms. Moore. After waiting two full hours and awaiting the time to see her mom; the doctor walked in holding a metal clipboard and wearing a pair of thin glasses.

"O.K. Ms. Stacy the results are in. After giving your mother our MC347 diagnoses test, we found that she has been infected with acute breast cancer "he explained.

"Oh shit, how bad is it Doc please tell me? She cried. "

Well she's in the third stage of the disease and surgery is a major factor. The procedure is quick and we may have to go in again," the doctor explained calmly.

"Yes, I understand. Can we see her?" she cried.

"Of course, just remember that she's weak and needs her rest too. She'll be free to go home in a few weeks," he stated convincingly.

"Thanks, I'll be in contact," Stacy said as she went to visit her mom. After several hours of visiting, Stacy and the kids prepared to leave until the surgery was finished.

Upon exiting the hospital Tee-Tee and Stacy talked over a quick blunt break. "Girl how have you been doing, how was your date?" Tee asked smiling.

"It was nice. Damon spent the night after a nice dinner. I sure appreciate you watching the kids too," Stacy spoke.

"It's cool sis. I love them two crazy kids. Anyhow, y'all look nice together," Tee-Tee commented.

"Thanks. He's trying to hold up…" Before she could finish her cell phone rang with a call from Damon. "O.K. Tee I'll catch ya later, this is him on the phone now," she whispered leaving the hospital.

On the phone Damon asked how her mother was doing and also asked to see her. Stacy declined the offer due to it being late and her having the kids. Damon understood as they made plans for breakfast the next morning.

Laying alone in her bed Stacy felt a fury of emotions. She worried about her mother, relationship, and her future as a parent. As she dozed off into a deep sleep several questions went unanswered until morning.

Upon waking up, Damon had ordered Stacy's favorite breakfast meal from a diner in Canton. He was extra excited this morning and couldn't wait to get to the house. Before pulling up to the block, he phoned to let her know to open the door.

"Ookkkkaaay," Stacy frantically said as she woke up to prep herself for a forgotten about breakfast. Once she fixed herself up she quickly rushed to the door to greet her guest.

The kids played in the living room as the sounds of a male voice alerted them. They rushed to see Damon and to invite him to play. He made a promise to join them later after breakfast was finished. As they sat at the table he placed the meal onto plates while she and he talked briefly.

She reached for a glass of orange juice and ice to drink. Seconds later she finished the drink only to find something unusual inside her glass. Placing her fingers inside to retrieve the object, she noticed a huge ring.

"What is this Damon?" she shouted.

"This is the ring that I need you to wear for the rest of your life. If you accept then we could replace your old one with this one, and you can wear the one Joey got you as a special necklace," he suggested smiling.

Stacy stood up in shock as her mind drifted back to the night Joey proposed to her. She was happy but conflicted at the same time, 'Am I wrong for feeling this way? Joey would want the best for us wouldn't he?'"

Then after forgetting where she was and how serious this moment was, she responded. "Of course, I'll give it a try, Boo" she said as she hugged him.

The pair told the children the news as Stacy called her best friend to let her know as well. Finally, someone has come into her life to give it more meaning and she couldn't wait to talk to her mom later at the hospital.

Things were coming together as she really thought hard about leaving the city forever. Maybe this was her big chance to readjust in another environment. The kids were about to start school and Chicago might be the best location to learn and grow in...

Chapter Twelve

It had been several weeks since Damon's proposal and Ms. Moore's admittance into the hospital. After two surgeries, her recovery was in question along with her health. The doctor had requested that another quick surgery procedure to remove the cyst and remaining cancer in her breast. Once Stacy was informed and agreed to let them operate, she was told that she'd be notified immediately after the process.

Stacy was concerned about the level of strength Ms. Moore lacked after their last visit. While she described the past events in her life like the engagement,

Ms. Moore could barely stay focused or awaken. This is what prompted the doctor to further examine the situation.

During the surgery, Stacy, Damon, and Tee-Tee all waited in the small room along with the twins. For six hours they paced back and forth as their hearts beat faster from anticipation. Finally, doctor Amin walked out removing his gloves and face guard. Locating the family, he brought them together and told them the bad news.

"I'm sorry Stacy, but the operation was a failure. Removing the cyst caused internal bleeding which we couldn't stop in time," he said with a blank face.

"What happened is she going to be alright?" she asked as the rest stood by.

"I'm sorry, but we lost her, she passed form at 11:37am. We tried everything that we could to save her. The cancer was eating her alive from the inside. The procedure was tricky and her strength came and went.

We're so terribly sorry about the loss of your mother. I'll leave you to mourn and I'll prepare for any arrangements needed," Doctor Amin explained slowly.

Stacy fell to her knees in tears as Damon tried to calm her down. The thoughts and reality sunk in like quicksand and took a complete emotional toll on her.

"Not my mom! Please not my mom! Damn, first my daddy and now this? Why me? Why me Lord?" Stacy cried while questioning herself.

Tee-Tee dropped to the floor to help calm her down and to reassure her that she wasn't alone. Once Stacy regained control the group headed home to talk and plan for the funeral service. As they entered the house Damon explained that he had to leave, but would return later that night.

Tee-Tee vowed to stay until then to help comfort the twins and Stacy, "It's going to be alright girl," she assured her. "Just stay strong we need you."

"I'm trying, but it seems like I'm cursed or something," she replied.

"You're not cursed, it's just God's plan taking it's course," Tee said.

"First my dad, then Joey and Kim, now my mom Tee?" Stacy said.

"I know baby, but at times like this we must find the good things in our life to be thankful for," Tee said.

"I guess," Stacy cried quietly.

"Yeah, you got two wonderful children and a man who loves you. That's all the family you need to grow, Boo," Tee-Tee stated.

They both cried and laughed the entire night as they reminisced about Ms. Moore and their life. Around 12am in the morning Damon showed up with flowers and ice cream prepared to take over the watch. Lying in the bed Stacy rolled over to talk to Damon who watched T.V. focused.

"Boo, I think we should move to Chicago this fall after the funeral," she suggested.

"Huh? You think that's a good idea? All of your family and friends are here," he said.

"Yeah, but I'm ready to start a new life and I trust that you'll treat me right," she said.

"Of course, I will," he said.

"I could open a store down there and have Tee help run the store here," she explained.

"How about we just take it day by day, Ma," he answered. Deep inside he knew that first she needed to mourn and plan for the burial of Ms. Moore. So, all the energy and time she had, needed to be directed on that task.

Over the next few days Stacy did all that she could to send her mom off in style. The church was called Greater Grace and the pastor was someone who had preached the word for over a decade. Everyone was welcomed to the services as Ms. Moore was laid to rest in a cream and gray casket wearing a peach colored dress.

The children were watched by Tee-Tee who showed support along with Damon. As the members of the church and community visited the casket, Stacy greeted them all in tears.

In the middle of the ceremony the twins had no idea that granny wasn't alive. "Ma, Ma!!! Tell Granny to get up please!!!" they begged quietly in the front row.

This was a lot for Stacy to take in as she fell to the ground in tears. Damon rushed to aid in the attempt to keep her strong while the pastor spoke respectfully.

Suddenly, in the back of the church Rondo appeared to pay his respect to the family. He was spotted by Stacy as he waved to acknowledge her looking. Since he was family, she calmly motioned for him to join them in the front row.

After several hours the service was ending as folks headed to the cemetery for the final preparation. On their way out the church Rondo was forcefully bumped by two men.

"Damn nigga, do I know you?" Rondo asked as everyone looked.

"Of course you do, we've been a fan of your work for years. Allow me to introduce ourselves. This is Detective Freeman and I'm Detective Ross. We're the leading officials on Doc, Joey, Kim, and Ricky's caseloads," he explained.

"Well that's good to know, but as you can see I'm here to show compassion to the family. I'll catch y'all at a later time," Rondo joked.

"Oh trust me, we know all about you and the Fenkell Boyz crime wave. And just to let you know we got the ransom money and believe me Ricky will want revenge. So, if you don't want to help us, cool, if you change your mind, here's my card," Detective Ross suggested.

"Oh yeah, I'm straight detectives. Enjoy your day," Rondo smirked.

Before walking away the two detectives noticed Stacy with Damon. "Ms. Moore it's good to see that you're up and moving. Sorry about the loss of your mother. She seemed like a well-rounded woman," Detective Freeman spoke.

"Thank you both, but coming to pay respect is one thing and harassing people is another," she sadly said.

Without any further questions Damon quickly grabbed her and headed toward the limo with the family.

"In due time partner things will reveal themselves. Keep a tail on Rondo and figure out who the new boy toy is also. Hmmm, I wonder who the father of the twins turned out to be?" Detective Ross asked.

"Good question, however, shit looks weird around here. I'll catch ya at the office to debrief you later," Detective Freeman replied walking away.

While the funeral moved to the cemetery, everyone followed to witness the release of the white doves and to say their final goodbye's....

Chapter Thirteen

A full month has passed since the departure of Ms. Moore and summer was in full swing as June ushered July in.

Stacy and Damon had been spending a lot of time as a couple while the healing process was ongoing. In the hood things were quiet as Tee-Tee stayed supportive and Rondo controlled the streets.

This weekend would be extremely hot outside as 'Brick-Bottom's' local rap group celebrated their 4th annual 3-day bash. The celebration included a huge picnic at 'Rouge Park' along with a party on Saturday and a car show on Sunday. Special guest from around the globe would appear along with celebrities from the music industry. There would be live entertainment from the local music groups and star performance by Bun-B and Plies.

Rondo had alliance with the entire Westside and planned to attend the events with the crew. He got dressed wearing Gucci from head to toe and by sporting a jewelry set worth over $250,000 grand. Everyone showed up at the 3-day event so he pulled out his cream BMW 760 with 24inch Dalvin rims.

To keep security tight, several crew members followed his every move in a super stretch Denali XL. Over the next two days, he would show out in expensive cars, bikes, and trucks. This was his way of letting the streets know that his worth was unlimited.

Missing Doc and still in mourning, he had the trunk of his 86 Grand National airbrushed with his portrait. The events were well planned as the D.J.

spanned a variety of tunes and several crews networked

throughout. The women wore their best attire in search of

the boys with the toys and money to blow.

On the last day of the picnic everyone met at

Chene Park for the Eastside vs. Westside car show. Even

though Rondo didn't enter the event he still showed up to

support. Pulling up in his B.M.W. he was greeted by C-

Rock and Kirk and motioned where to VIP Park.

The entire parking lot and park was filled with

multiple cars of all sorts. They had Impala's, Chevy's,

Corvettes, Trucks and Bikes all tricked out in unique

ways.

On the other side of the park several eastside

crews gathered in large and small groups. One particular

crew was surrounding Jeff and Tik giving them praise for

their cars. Jeff drove a '77' drop top Bonneville with six

T.V.'s and 26inch rims. The inside of the car was yellow

while the outside was dark purple with yellow stripes. He had the words "Kobe" stitched in the seats and "Balling" on the headrest.

Tik arrived in a burnt orange '7' box Chevy Malibu on 28inch rims that spanned. The seats were leather cream colored and the doors lifted up like airplane wings. People gathered around surveying the cars and trucks while the judges checked for flaws.

Jeff sat in a small lounge chair watching the crowd when, across the large park he saw something odd. A group of young men all sporting F.B.C. shirts were being flocked by several beautiful women.

"Damn, Tik they bad as hell," Jeff said.

"Where at?" Tik asked.

"Over there by the B.M.W." Jeff spoke.

"Yeah, she cold blooded with the thong showing," Tik replied.

"Dog, that look like that nigga Rondo she talking to," Jeff said.

Tik stood up to get a better view over the crowd. After focusing for several seconds, he had his verdict. "Damn fam that's ya mans, true that. What ya want to do?" he asked.

Jeff sat back and thought for a minute. Finally, after realizing that a shootout wouldn't be smart, he picked up the phone and called Ricky. Ricky was hanging out in the Miami's Over-Town Projects with a few locals. While sitting on his Rolls Royce his cell rang with a call from Jeff. "Talk to me," Ricky answered.

"What up doe, fam? Dig, you'll never believe where I am and who I spotted," Jeff said toying with him.

"Time is money little homie and I ain't got time to solve no riddles," Ricky replied.

"Cool, I feel ya. I'm at Chene Park at the car show and ya boy Rondo is up here straight stunting," he said.

"Oh yeah, handle that, then call me. Quarter Mill still stands" Ricky said.

"Fam, now aint a good time. Ya dig?" Jeff responded.

"What!!! Ok tell ya this. Keep him close by and don't fucking lose the nigga. I'll be down there in the morning before noon. Call Tank and tell him to be ready for plan B," Ricky demanded loudly.

Once they ended the conversation Jeff and Tik laid back to keep an eye on Rondo. Since the car show was getting underway, Jeff had his girlfriend take his car while he drove hers. He knew that tailing him in a fancy car would bring too much attention. So, Tik and him jumped in her Malibu with their guns and patiently waited.

The weather was 90 degrees as they sat across the parking lot unnoticed by Rondo or his crew. Time had stood still for no one as the car show came to its final stages of the evening. In the center of the park on the medium size stage, Pone and Rell prepared to announce this year's winners. To everyone's surprise the Westside won by a small margin. The Schoolcraft Boys came in 1st place with their '69' Drop Top G.T.O. with 30inch rims. In 2nd place was Tape's '88' Caprice on 32inch rims with Lambo doors. The crowd agreed as the decisions were made and for the rest of the night both sides chilled out violence free.

Around 9:30pm Rondo had the urge to grab something to eat. He motioned for the crew to round up so that they could head to the 'Coliseum Bar' to relax. While the crew members mounted up in multiple vehicles, Jeff and Tik did the same. Pulling out onto Jefferson St. the two followed several cars behind to keep their tail.

Once they arrived at the topless bar everyone entered with intentions on eating and blowing money fast. Inside the bar women dance around in their sexiest thongs and high heel shoes. The entire scene was exotic, as a huge variety of beautiful women singles out clients.

Rondo sat at the back table by the exit door, along with two of his boys. Once they were seated a cute petite waitress came to take their orders. She was 5 foot 7 and wore a short French maid outfit and sported long black hair. Rondo liked what he saw so he flirted while ordering several bottles of champagne.

Since the bar was packed with ballers, The Fenkell Boyz played their part by throwing unlimited dollar bills at the dancers. Suddenly, while Rondo was talking to an exotic dancer and stuffing money into her lace thong; the petite waitress came back to bring another round of champagne.

"Excuse me baby, but here are your drinks," she shouted.

"What drinks? We already tight sexy," Rondo spoke in her ear. The waitress looked around at the bar manager confused. The slim woman walked over to the table to explain the situation.

"Oh, sorry handsome, but these drinks were sent over by those two gentlemen over there," she said while pointing at Jeff and Tik.

"Who them niggas?" Rondo asked with an evil look.

Rondo had never saw Jeff or Tik before that night, so he was anxious and aware of the gesture. Once he started to send his crew over to greet them, the two casually ducked out using the crowd as their shields.

"Who are those niggas shorty? Aye I'm cool on this shit, send it back," he yelled.

"But they gone, Boo," the waitress replied.

"Well you drink it. We cool, Ma," Rondo ended.

After the drinks were gone Rondo realized that the two dudes were most likely from the eastside. So, quickly, he sent a few dudes outside only to get word that the men had disappeared. He was upset and back inside the club he showed it, suspecting this could have been a hit or set up.

Filling up everyone's glasses, Rondo made a loud toast with his crew which caused major attention. He stood in the center of the table raising his glass while shouting drunkenly, "This my city and the Fenkell Boyz run shit! Rest in peace to my nigga Doc, who we love and miss. Fuck the eastside! If they want war or my life over some out of state niggas, fuck 'em come and get me!" Rondo said before drowning in champagne.

All the party goers looked on as they tried not to excite or become engaged in a bar brawl. Many of them just continued to throw money and watch the entertainment, especially knowing that everything Rondo

said he meant and could do....

Chapter Fourteen

The next day Ricky flew to Detroit and met up with Tank at the stash house.

"What it do, pimp?" Tank greeted.

"Got a little work to put in on the strength of my bro and seed," Ricky replied.

"I won't hold you up fam, dig this all that you ordered," Tank said while pointing at a huge box.

Ricky calmly opened and inspected every weapon inside it. "These are straight Tank. Thanks for the quick service. Your money is in the car," he spoke.

After paying several grand for a few handguns and assault weapons the meeting was over. While Jeff drove, Ricky arranged to have a few goons locate Rondo to settle the score. He wanted to kill Rondo himself for revenge of his family and he wanted to do it up close and personal.

Meanwhile, on the Westside Rondo awoke to a hangover and headache. He checked his phone for missed calls and starts to return a few of them. One call was from Stacy and another was from Candy.

Once he took a few pills, he dialed Stacy back first. "Hello?" she answered.

"What up doe sis?" Rondo said.

"Shit, just wanted to check on you," she said.

"I'm cool just getting up, fixing the hangover," he said.

"Yeah, I heard that you put on a show last night."

Rondo sat quiet on the other end as he mumbled under his breath. "Damn girl you always hearing some shit," he joked.

"Yeah and Tee-Tee told me that she saw Ricky in traffic," she said.

"Oh yeah, huh?" he responded.

"Yeah, so be careful because if he's in the city then he's up to no good," she stated.

"Good looking. I'm out fam, I'll call you later," he said while hanging up.

Rondo began to start his day by showering and getting dressed. His mind wasn't on the night before, but more of the fact that his enemy was lurking close to home. Word on the street had gotten out; that Ricky was the one behind the burning of Stacy's building. However, the revenge plot was coded due to the suspects fleeing town to lay low.

Putting on his vest Rondo grabbed his cell to call Candy back. Candy was the waitress from the bar last night. While talking to her they made plans for him to pay a quick visit to the bar later. He had a few stops to make prior too, but arranged to pick her up after hours.

Knowing that business had to continue and not fucking a new chick wasn't an option. Rondo stayed focus on the task at hand by calling his crew to locate Ricky.

Throughout the day neither one of the gentlemen rested easily at all. The ongoing beef was about to come to an end no matter the cost or consequences. At the room Ricky watched T.V. as he patiently waited for the call from Tik saying he found Rondo. Inside the large room Jeff rolled a blunt and talked on his cell.

Suddenly, a call came in from Damon requesting to speak to Ricky.

"What it do D-Man?" Jeff answered.

"Put Ricky on the phone," he demanded.

Quickly Jeff motioned for Ricky to get the phone then exited the room to go smoke. "Who this?" Ricky asked.

"Listen, I thought we had an agreement about your visits to Detroit," he said.

"Yeah, but sometimes a man gotta do what a man's gotta do," Ricky said.

"Chasing this vendetta will end up in a blood bath and all money will stop," Damon explained.

"How you know I was here?" Ricky asked.

Damon thought first, but chose not to give up his source. Truthfully, Stacy had called and told him out of fear of something happening to Rondo or her. "Just know that I got eyes everywhere Ricky. Just like I know about the hit on my girl and the burning of her business."

"Well, I just recently found out that you were fucking ole girl. She a live wire so be careful. Out of respect I called all orders off toward her, but ya boy needs to answer for his own actions," Ricky explained smoothly.

"Huh, since you wanna play Scarface. I'll say this to you and him. Don't fuck with my money or my patience!!!!" Damon shouted.

"Cool down fam, this ain't about us or business. Let me handle this shit and I'm gone. Catch ya later, the other line beeping," Ricky tried to state.

"This is my final warning Ricky, don't try me!" Damon said as he hung up the phone.

On the other line was Tik, ready to give the latest on finding his target. "This me, talk" Ricky demanded agitated.

"Aye, dig this real quick. I just got a call from my bitch Candy from the bar. She said that Rondo agreed to pick her up after work," Tik spoke.

"Cool, I'll meet y'all up there at 1:30am so lay low and call me when he pull up. That's when I'll take him out for good," he ended excited.

As Rondo made his rounds with his two boys; time started to pass quickly. He hadn't got a word from anyone on the streets about Ricky. Inside he started to think that maybe Tee-Tee didn't see him in traffic or Stacy was pulling a stay alert tactic. So, around 1:00am he decided to head to the strip club to wait for Candy to get off work.

Pulling up to the crowded bar he valet the ride and all three entered to relax. Since he was a made nigga and regular of the establishment, security quietly allowed the crew to keep their weapons. Inside the lavish bar Rondo was seated in his favorite seat in the back by the exit door. Candy spotted him and quickly went to greet and service their table. "Hey boo, you early. You couldn't wait to see me huh?" she stated smiling.

"You know it sexy. My day ended a little sooner than I expected so I said fuck it, why not have a drink until you get off," he replied.

"It's cool, Boo. How about I bring you your favorite drinks then I'll catch you in the parking lot later," Candy suggested.

Once the drinks were delivered to the table, Candy snuck into the dressing room to use her cell phone. Nervously she dialed Tik number to alert him that Rondo had showed up early. Tik immediately headed to the bar to post up outside until Ricky could show up. About 20 minutes later, Tik and Vaughn spotted Rondo's car in the valet section. They called Candy to come outside so that she could retrieve the 5 grand promised to her for the setup. Placing the money inside her Gucci handbag, calmly she strolled back into the club.

Next, Tik phoned Ricky while watching the vehicle. "What up doe fam, we here and dog inside two-deep," Tik explained.

"Alright, load up and stay put. We 10 minutes away," Ricky demanded.

Back inside the bar the DJ announced last call for drinks as everyone rushed the bar. It was almost 2am, so Rondo searched the crowd for Candy as 'Yo Gotti' hit '5 star chic' blasted throughout the speakers. After searching for several minutes, he figured that maybe she was waiting in the parking lot. Together the three headed for the door to leave, when suddenly Rondo changed the routine.

"Dig, y'all go and grab the car and I'mma slide out the back door for a second," he suggested. In his mind, he remembered a few nights ago when the two strangers sent him free drinks. If they were there to kill him or warn him he had no idea. He had tried to investigate, but when he sent his crew to see about them they had vanished unnoticed. So, for safety reasons he played the side door in case they showed up.

Once the two crew members exited the bar to wait for the valet to bring the car around; Tik and Vaughn slowly took their guns off safety and strolled toward the two waiting men.

Ricky sat in the car with Jeff and waited until he saw Rondo. Walking up into the club, Tik and Vaughn didn't see Rondo and they gave the two men a heads up.

They quickly reached for their weapons being that they remembered the face of Tik from before. "It's a hit!!!!" one crew member shouted.

Seconds later Tik and Vaughn fired shots from their pistols, hitting the two men before they could retrieve their weapons.

Several shots rang out and people ran for cover. Rondo was coming around the building when he paused from hearing gunshots. When he finally focused in the direction of the noise, he observed both of his boys laying in blood. He also observed Tik and Vaughn trying to flee the scene to their car.

Instantly Rondo gave chase unnoticed through the crowd and caught the two jumping into their vehicle. While Tik rushed to put the car into drive, Vaughn reloaded his weapon. Too late, within that split-second Rondo ran up on the car firing several shots into it.

Bulletw flew from the gun, leaving shells from the .45 Caliber spread all over the graveled parking lot. Rondo had a good aim as each bullet met its mark. Two shots hit Tik in the head, while another three tore through the neck and chest of Vaughn.

Preparing to leave them lying in a pool of blood, Rondo started to run to his car. On the other side of the parking lot, Ricky jumped out of the car, leaving Jeff behind.

"Damn, this shit done got messy! Stay here and keep the car running," Ricky demanded.

Next, he headed toward Rondo who was not expecting any more drama. The closer that he got the more anxious Ricky was to complete his mission. With the gun in hand, Ricky aimed at Rondo's head while running up to his car.

Out of the corner of Rondo's eye he quickly noticed Ricky charging full speed ahead. He then raised his .45 caliber. The two then engaged in a gun battle for several seconds which indeed seemed like hours. At close range shots were fired in all directions as both men raced for cover.

Rondo hid behind a large dumpster in the alley, while Ricky hid on the side of a Lexus 430. The crowd had thinned out and sirens from police cars could be heard getting closer.

In hiding Rondo looked down at his feet as fatigue started to set in. "Shit ahhhh shit!" he moaned quietly. Rondo had just realized that he was shot in the lower stomach and lower back beneath the vest as the pain set in he started to feel his legs stiffening up, so in one motion he reversed the clip in the gun.

Once Ricky stopped hearing gunshots he checked to see if Jeff was still around. Then he took a deep breath while he searched for any gunshot wounds. After realizing that he wasn't hit, he took another deep breath to prepare for another exchange of gun fire. Peeping under the car Ricky could see Rondo lying wounded. Quickly, he jogged over to the spot where Rondo laid ready to end this long war. Rondo had begun to fade in and out of consciousness when he saw a blurry vision of Ricky.

"Yeah motherfucker! This is for my brother and son!" Ricky yelled before pulling the trigga.

At the same time Rondo had saved just enough energy to squeeze the trigger of his gun. Instantly both men were hit by each other's bullet fatally wounding them.

Ricky fell to the ground from a lucky shot that hit him directly in the heart. While Rondo had faded away from another single shot to the right eye. As both men lay dead along with the other four crew members, Jeff slowly pulled up to check for life. Once he verified that everyone was dead he then pulled off quickly, before the cops showed up.

Approximately 30 minutes after the violent showdown at the bar, multiple cops surrounded the crime scene in search for answers. A few seconds later Detectives Ross and Freeman arrived to take lead of the investigation. "Look at this crazy shit. It's two o'clock in the morning and yet we have another homicide" Detective Ross said.

"Yeah, another day in the city partner. Let's get out and check the details," Detective Ross replied back hastily.

Exiting the Crown Vic both men headed toward the uniformed officer and crime scene.

"Hello Detectives, I'm SGT Lawson, the first in charge in this district," the stocky gentlemen spoke.

"What do we have here, Sarge?" Detectives Ross asked.

"It seems like the wild-wild west was brought to Motown. A few witnesses told me that this was an ambush of some sort. These two guys here were shot on sight and as you can see, they still have their weapons on them. Now these two over here were shot inside the car from, I'm assuming this guy here," he said pointing at Rondo. "We found .45 caliber casings on the ground and as you can see he's holding a .45 caliber. As for this one lying next to the shooter, today just wasn't his lucky day.

It seems that he somehow was hit close range by this dudes weapon. Once the meat wagon arrives I'll have them check for I.D.'s" the SGT spoke again.

The detectives quickly noticed Rondo and Ricky's faces as they looked at each other with a smirk. "I can't believe this," Detective Ross said. "Excuse me SGT but there won't be any need to identify these two gangsters. We know them personally and now this little massacre has just come to light," Detective Freeman replied.

"Ok, but I'll still follow protocol and do an I.D. check on all six to notify next of kin," the SGT suggested.

"Cool, you handle that and get back with us," Detective Freeman agreed.

After helping collect evidence the detectives bagged and tagged the bodies. Shortly afterwards they headed back to the office to resume paperwork and to focus on the case.

"Well buddy this might be the end of the long-term beef," Detective Ross said.

"Of course, only time will tell," Freeman said.

"Quite ironic how this all played out over the past few years, huh?" Ross stated.

"Gotta love an open and shut case load though," Freeman said.

"Too bad that all this blood had to be shed over a mere love affair," Ross said.

"Ha, ha, pussy has been the number one cause of deaths since the early 1700s," Detective Freeman joked.

"On a different note partner, we have a lot of work to do and the T.V. reporters are out front waiting for a statement," he said.

"Well let's go deliver the news to the city and hopefully peace will be restored," the detective said.

While the detectives continued to do their jobs and focus on the streets; In Chicago Damon got word of the shootout at the bar. He quietly arranged for a drive down to the city and called Stacy to check on her. Stacy was upset and could barely talk about the current situation pertaining to Rondo. Damon understood that somehow she was losing everyone that meant something to her.

So on his drive down, he phoned Jeff and Mr. A to set up a meeting. He wanted to seize the war and still do business with both sides. As for the Miami crew Ricky's older brother took control and met with Damon later.

Things had taken a dramatic turn as the entire city of Detroit and Miami mourned the loss of many fallen soldiers. At the meeting, a deal was reached and truce was called with the visions of prosperity. Damon was the kingpin and Jeff ran the Eastside boys.

On the Westside Mr. A recruited another high ranked member of the F.B.C. to control this territory. In memory of his son he still had his grandchildren, whom he would one, day groom to run the family business. Life is hard and the future is never promised, so Damon and

Stacy took advantage of every moment....

Chapter Fifteen

A year had passed and Tee-Tee and Stacy were at the cemetery with the twins visiting their loved ones. It was hard to believe that it had been seven years since the death of Joey and Kim.

Over the last year Stacy and Damon were married at a church in Detroit. This was actually, the same church that Ms. Moore was laid to rest at peacefully. The wedding was amazing and lavish and Tee-Tee had the privilege of being the Maid of Honor.

At the wedding both children played flower keepers and Damon spared no expense on the budget. At this point in Stacy's life she was finally happy and complete, but still mourned the loss of her loved ones.

"You okay, sis?" Tee-Tee asked concerned.

"Yeah girl, it's just crazy how my life took so many turns," Stacy replied.

"It's all a part of God's plan Cee-Cee. You overcame a lot of obstacles and now look at you. You're married with two wonderful children, plus you have me for a best friend," Tee-Tee joked.

"Hmmmm, you're right Tee. You've been a true friend from day one and I thank you for it," Stacy said.

"I know that I could never take Kim's place, but hey I'll try," again she joked.

As the two conversed the twins laid flowers and played around the grave sites of their dad.

"Another thing Tee-Tee that I wanted to share with you is that I truly appreciate you running the store. I know Rome don't like you working and I promise that I'll hire a manager a.s.a.p." Stacy explained sadly.

"It's alright girl, we got your back. You just focus on your business in Chicago and enjoy your life down there. It is boring now that you're all settled in and stuff," Tee said.

"Ha, ha, don't worry child, I'm only a few hours away and you already know the kids love them some Aunt Tee-Tee" Stacy reassured smiling.

Once they finished talking Stacy asked for a quick minute to be alone with Ms. Moore. Tee-Tee understood and took the twins back to the car to wait. While alone with the tombstones, Stacy began to talk out loud to her mother. "Hey Ma, I just wanted to talk to you for a second before I left to walk to Joey's place of rest. I miss you so much along with Daddy. I wish you two could be here to share this life with me. As angels, you look down and help protect our family from evil. I thank you for the blessings and for sending me a good man. Hopefully, I'm making you both proud and I promise to be the best parent and wife that you raised. There's still a lot to learn in life and with you two watching over me, I know I'll be alright. I love you and please keep me close," Stacy spoke sadly.

Once she finished talking to Ms. Moore she then slowly walked a few rows over to visit Joey's grave site. Standing inches away from his huge headstone and picture, she began to speak softly. "Hey baby, I miss you soooo much and love you just the same. I'm sorry for putting you in this situation and only pray that you can forgive me. I had to move on with my life Joey, this was the only way that I could heal. I hope that you're happy for me and truly understand. He's a good to me and our daughter. Joey, you showed me so much and introduced me to an entirely new lifestyle. No one could ever replace the love I have for you inside my heart. Life is a roller coaster baby and as of now I'm going upwards. I really wanted to come here today to express my love for you. You a wonderful man Joey, the best I ever had and for that I'll love you always," Stacy ended as she kissed the headstone of Joey.

While walking back to the car in tears, she was met by Tee-Tee who was on her cell. "I'll call you back, Boo," she spoke into the cell as she hung up. "You Okay, Princess?" Tee-Tee asked concerned.

"Yeah, just a little emotional sis. I needed this visit to ease my mind," Stacy explained.

"It's cool girl, just relax and let's go grab a bite to eat, the kids are starving," Tee-Tee suggested.

Suddenly before getting into the car, Stacy turned to Tee-Tee and looked directly into her eyes. "Tee, can I tell you something?" Stacy said.

"Sure, what's the matter Cee?" Tee said.

"I've been holding a secret in my life and it's weighing heavy on my heart," Stacy said sadly.

"Your secret is safe with me, Boo. I'm your girl, your sister and your best friend. I promise you can trust me," Tee confirmed.

"Tee, listen, I'm not a bad person. I just made some poor choices in my life," she said.

"And?" Tee said.

"The twins have separate fathers," she said.

"Huh, what do you mean?" Tee asked.

"Joetta is Joey's and Tyrik is Terrance's son," Stacy confessed.

"What! You're kidding me!" Tee-Tee responded. Tee-Tee had a blank look on her face as she tried to stay non-bias.

"Nobody knows Tee, not even my mom or Joey's parents," she stated. "Oh my God girl, this is weird. What you gonna do when the twins get older and start asking questions. Don't you think they need to know the truth?" Tee-Tee asked again.

"Yes they do Tee, but this will cause a major separation in their lives," she said.

"I agree, but still," Tee said.

"It's cool Sis. Trust me they'll know at the right time. So, until then this is between you and me. I just needed someone close to know in case something happens to me," Stacy said calmly.

"Jesus thanks for trusting me and I'll always be there for all of y'all," Tee-Tee assured.

You're a true friend Tee. I just hope this doesn't spiral out of control in the future. When they grow up the truth will push them apart. I just pray that they'll stay family," Stacy said.

"Only time will tell sis, only time will tell," Tee-Tee said while shaking her head.

After their conversation, they jumped into the car and headed off into the sunset to enjoy a quick dinner. Stacy knew that one day all she had done in her past would come to light. She just prayed that the

consequences wouldn't outweigh the rewards.

So, until then life with Damon would have to be

the beginning of a new her. This time her loyalty would

definitely help her escape betrayal...

THE END

QUESTIONS:

1) At what point did Stacy become a better person or woman?

2) How would you handle Stacy's situation about the twins?

3) Do you think that Rondo went too far for revenge?

4) Could the beef between Ricky and Rondo been solved without mischief?

5) Did Doc deserved to be killed?

6) Did Rondo handle his power correctly?

7) Do you think that Stacy should have told the kids about their dads?

8) Do you believe that Tee-Tee gave good advice?

9) How did the passing away of Ms. Moore affect Stacy?

10) Do you believe that Stacy made the right decision by marrying Damon and revealing her secret?

Book Cover:

It had been several years since the murder-suicide by Big-T on J-rock. While Stacy had survived the vicious attempt on her life and was now blessed with twins. Figuring out who fathered the twins would be a breeze; but avoiding the drama in her life would prove a harder task. As Stacy tries to put her life back on track, Rondo, the twins God-father, has another plan. While living in Detroit can be hard, Stacy strives hard to rebuild her life and someday re-find love. Thanks to the help of her best friend Tee-Tee her options widen with experience. There's only one thing that can stop her from being successful and that one thing is always lurking within her. Will Stacy make her dreams come true or will she let her past hinder her future, because true Loyalty never dies…